westland ltd

MY HUSBAND AND OTHER ANIMALS

Janaki Lenin has always had an interest in animals but living with Rom took it to the stratospheric level. They lived in the Madras Crocodile Bank for a few years, surrounded by thousands of crocodiles, snakes, turtles, and lizards. Rom and Janaki made documentaries about wildlife in wild places for a living.

When they moved to their farm in rural Tamil Nadu, Janaki thought it would be a perfect retreat after the many arduous months of filming. Instead, a whole new set of challenges popped up – from pesky tree frogs and adamant Russell's vipers to a dog-eating leopard. She thinks she's made her peace with the many wild creatures who have staked claim to their farm, but who knows what tomorrow may bring. Rom and Janaki live with four dogs, a pair of emus, a flock of geese, and a pig. It's her childhood dream come true.

Praise for *My Husband and Other Animals*

'With insight, verve, and deep feeling, Janaki Lenin writes about the creatures around her, from tree frogs and snakes to her dog and husband. Her essays are a delight to read.'

– George Schaller, wildlife biologist,
Wildlife Conservation Society, New York

'The legendary M. Krishnan set a near-impossible standard for nature and wildlife columnists. Janaki Lenin has got there with effortless ease and the added appeal of a very feminine sensibility tromping both barefoot and in the most rugged footwear.'

– Gopalkrishna Gandhi, former administrator,
diplomat, governor, and author

'I'm an ardent follower of the wildlife encounters – some threatening, some hilarious, some heartbreaking – of Janaki and Rom in jungles in India and around the world and read her weekly column with some envy, wishing I was with them.'

– Timeri N. Murari,
author of *The Taliban Cricket Club*

'Janaki Lenin explores the familiar and unfamiliar aspects of nature with a knowledgeable sense of humour and a sharp eye for detail. Her columns in *The Hindu* follow the tradition of Gerald Durrell but also wander off the beaten track, blending personal and scientific observations on India's diverse ecology and natural heritage.'

– Stephen Alter, author of *Elephas Maximus:*
A Portrait of the Indian Elephant

'Janaki Lenin has honed a rare talent to be both engagingly accessible and scientifically authoritative. She is fast becoming our home-grown David Quammen.'

– Pradip Krishen, author of *Trees of Delhi*

My Husband and Other Animals

JANAKI LENIN

ⱳ

westland ltd
61, II Floor, Silverline Building, Alapakkam Main Road, Maduravoyal,
Chennai 600 095
93, I Floor, Sham Lal Road, Daryaganj, New Delhi 110 002

First published in India by westland ltd 2012

10 9 8 7 6 5 4 3

ISBN: 978-93-81626-72-6

Illustrations by Gynelle Alves

Typeset in10/14 pts. PalmSprings by SÜRYA, New Delhi

Printed at Radha Press, Sahibabad

Contents

viii | CONTENTS

Foreword

It seems these days as if people have forgotten their biological roots or lost interest in animals and plants or been led astray by modern attention-grabbers, such as celebrities, computer games and Facebook. The biodiversity of Planet Earth apparently doesn't matter any more, and this concerns me greatly.

It's clear that Janaki Lenin feels the same. Trying her hand at documentary film-making, she defied the television executives who wanted human personalities to dominate the screen in programmes about animals. And I am glad she did, as her rebelliousness gave impetus to her column in *The Hindu*, on which this book is based.

This delightful compendium goes a long way to filling the current gap in popular writing on the subjects of wildlife and natural history.

Like Gerald Durrell, my late husband and one of her heroes, Janaki demonstrates a refreshing breadth of interest in and knowledge of natural history, linking nature to her spouse, to all human endeavour, to God and the Universe!

The topics with which Janaki enchants her readers are incredibly diverse and always fascinating. Virgin birth in reptiles, how to train animals (including husbands), invasions by tree frogs and egrets, the innocuous-looking, but pain-inflicting devil nettle and the fabulous *makara* and fearsome *kirtimukha* of Hindu mythology are just a few of her themes.

More than this, Janaki, again like Gerald, uses humour, storytelling and an easy, gentle style to remind us of the links between humans and the other species on the planet. It is upon these relationships that civilization rests, although few admit it or even recognize it today. But think about it ... from domestication of animals and plants, to love of the land, to inspiration derived from the intricacy, grandeur and beauty of nature, these connections make us humans what we are.

If our species is to persist, severing these connections is not possible, although, given our track record with the natural world, we seem to be trying hard to do so!

Janaki asks, '... what compels us humans to gobble and destroy our way through Earth's resources until there is no tomorrow?' The answer is that we have forgotten how we became human beings, how we evolved with and depended upon other species.

Janaki asks, 'Are we hell-bent on sending this unique life-sustaining planet to Saturn, the haunted house of Hindu astrology?' At present the appalling answer is certainly yes, but it doesn't have to be. If we can collectively recall our evolutionary history, acknowledge our dependence on the ecosystem functions sustained by biodiversity and behave as if we believe in it, then Earth ... and we ... will survive.

7 June 2012 **LEE DURRELL**

Genesis

'My Husband and Other Animals' began as a short article for the Madras Crocodile Bank's newsletter, *Herpinstance*. I wrote about the many little creepy crawlies that shared our home with us on a farm, near a town called Chengalpattu, not far from Chennai city. The article was called 'Creepy Crawly Household'.

A few months later, K.V. Sudhakar of the Madras Naturalists' Society asked permission to reprint this article in the Society's newsletter, *Blackbuck*. I said I could do better. I expanded on the theme – chronicling the slow colonization of our home and garden by various creatures. I called the piece 'Life on the Edge of the Scrub'.

Perhaps a year or so later, Prerna Singh Bindra used the article for Air Deccan's in-flight magazine, *Simplifly*. Then she wanted to include it in her anthology of wildlife writing, *Voices in the Wilderness*. While I was editing the piece to the required word length, the title occurred to me in a flash: 'My Husband and Other Animals'.

At the same time, S. Theodore Baskaran edited a collection of articles from the Madras Naturalists' Society's newsletter called *The Sprint of the Blackbuck*. It was embarrassing to have two anthologies print the same article under different titles in the same year, but it was beyond my control. I didn't know about *The Sprint of the Blackbuck* anthology until it was too late. No other article I've written has been requested for reprinting so many times.

Meanwhile, I quit all administrative jobs to concentrate on writing. I wanted to work on a book, but Rom advised me to write a column. 'About what?' I demanded querulously. Then one bright summer morning in 2010, the idea firmly took root to write about our lives and adventures. But who would publish such a column? To my complete surprise, Mukund Padmanabhan at *The Hindu* liked the idea and the rest is here for you to read.

I write about Rom's growing-up years, his experiences before we met, our lives together, Rom teaching me about the wild, rearing pets, and observations of wild creatures, plants and much more. I embraced the expanse of natural history, and in the process of writing, learnt a lot.

Hope you enjoy reading this collection as much as I loved writing it.

The Curse of the Tree Frog

If I thought the two-storey house Rom and I built on our farm in the shelter of a magnificent banyan tree was for us humans, I was sadly mistaken. During the first summer, I was pleased to see a few tree frogs make themselves at home. With their dainty feet tucked under their bodies and their large, beseeching eyes, I didn't begrudge them tenancy. But then the word obviously got out, and great-great-grandchildren, cousins twice-removed and grandmothers-in-law moved in too.

Soon every ledge, book, mug, and framed picture was occupied. Some moved into the soap dispenser of the washing machine, others into the wash basin outlet pipe, yet others ensconced themselves in the cistern of the flush tank, and many more were neatly tucked in the narrow space between wall and cupboard. In a fit of benevolence, they left us a bit of space to live our lives.

Half a decade earlier, I had spent a year in the city and couldn't afford a cat or dog as a companion. Instead I adopted a petite tree frog. In the pantry where he lived, I left a basin of water for his ablutions and the light on at night to attract insects for his meals. It was a responsibility-free relationship; the pet frog didn't expect me to walk, feed, or train him. His entire existence was eked out in that tiny humid room. Although we didn't spend cuddly moments together, I felt some comfort having the tree frog around. All was well until one day he was killed by a falling book. I felt terrible.

The karmic offshoot was that now the Curse of the Tree Frog was upon me. If it was just space the frogs wanted in our new home, I would have held my peace. But they angled their bottoms strategically outwards and indiscriminately targeted counters, tables, towels, and even dinner plates. In some rooms, dried frog piss streaked the walls. Sitting on the toilet was a special gauntlet, for huddling unseen below the rim were more frogs. They played 'BOO' with unwary guests by slapping themselves on the most vulnerable part of the body. One big mamma frog drizzled pee on anyone unfortunate enough to switch on the overhead bathroom light. Tired of having to use a dark bathroom, towels stinking of froggie runs, and cleaning plates several times a day, we declared an admittedly gentle war on the leaping blighters.

We spent one Sunday catching all 289 of them in plastic bags and releasing them in neighbouring wells. But it was all for naught. Tree frogs may be tiny creatures, but they sure know their way around. Their fine-tuned homing instincts brought them back even before the last one was removed. Within 24 hours, they were all back at their favourite spots; it was as if they had never left. I bowed to their superior talents.

Several sneaked through a small gap under the door of the corner cupboard in the kitchen, and staked ownership of wok, pressure cooker, and blender bowls. Once when I was frying garlic, there arose a strong stench of . . . no, it couldn't be . . . *tree frog piss*! It had taken me a million years to just peel a few garlic cloves, and I wasn't about to spend my remaining life peeling more. So I added extra spices to mask the odour. I can't be sure if the compliments that followed were the result of my expert cooking or that undercurrent of, shall we say, the chef's secret ingredient.

A Partridge by Any Other Name

I was showing a visitor around our farm when a bird flew up from the bamboo. I called it a ring-dove. The visitor corrected me. 'Nope, that's a Eurasian collared-dove.' This was the third time I had been corrected in the past few months. I felt wobbly as my hard-earned knowledge of bird identities became worthless; I could no longer just rattle off names. Imagine, one fine day, if everyone you knew began responding to completely new names.

Although Rom knew his birds well, he had long ago adopted a snobbish attitude in the presence of bird-people. In his exaggerated nasal New York accent, he referred to them variously as 'noisy, stinky boids' and 'good croc-chow'. In my current state of uncertainty, these jibes didn't help.

Since Salim Ali used the old bird names in his *Book of Indian Birds*, it was no use to me anymore. So I picked up the newer *A Field Guide to the Birds of India* by Krys Kazmierczak. I wished to see how many names I needed to relearn; the list was long and demoralizing. The familiar houbara bustard has become Macqueen's bustard; the sweet little lorikeet has transformed into a pedantic vernal hanging-parrot. Only a prissy Victorian could have changed white-breasted kingfisher to white-throated kingfisher. It may not be a true creature of the jungle, but still, jungle crow is the name we call the common, large, handsome, glossy, black bird. Now none of the bird books list this name; instead it is known as the large-billed crow. At least it is still a crow. Some others have been ignominiously torn from their families and lumped with others, like the brahminy myna which has morphed into the brahminy starling.

From where did they dredge up some of these names? For instance, the red avadavat, which sounds like a court order, was formerly the red munia. The descriptive streaked fantail-warbler became zitting cisticola, which sounds more like a counterfeit soft drink. What, may I ask, is wrong with the good old golden-backed woodpecker? It is now the common flameback.

The one name change that bothered me the most was the grey partridge. It was henceforth to be called grey francolin. What's the difference between 'partridge' and 'francolin'? In an effort to bring clarity to the bevy of African spurfowls, partridges and francolins, our own bird became enmeshed in an Afro-Asian name change extravaganza. In description, our partridges conform to francolins, but behaviourally, they are quite different. Francolins sit motionless on the ground when alarmed, and do not perch on trees or bushes. Our partridges usually run away, but if they have been busy pecking at the ground and don't notice you approaching, they can give you a cardiac arrest when all of them take off with a sudden, loud whirring of wings. They roost on small trees, bamboo and thorny bushes in our garden, sometimes in groups of up to eight birds. Their calls are atonal and reminiscent of a creaky pump dying for a shot of oil. So tell us, O Wise Twitchers, do we have a partridge or a francolin here?

This nightmare was unleashed by globetrotting bird-naming – sorry – birdwatching professionals. Their rationale was: there were too many English names for a single species of bird across its range. But to replace this chaos with names that are neither common nor even in English isn't the answer.

After much consultation with several bird aficionados in 2004, Ranjit Manakan and Aasheesh Pittie came up with a list which takes the middle path. But the foreign experts have largely ignored this tremendous effort. Since the process began, others have joined in to lift this whole enterprise to esoteric levels. For instance, should 'common' names have hyphens?

By the time I get up to speed with all the new names, they'll likely have changed twice over. My best bet is to learn the names in Greek or Latin.

Better still, get a life.

A Leopard Comes Calling

In June 2006, Karadi, our gorgeous, 45-kg German shepherd, went missing. We assumed he had been stolen and began an extensive search of the neighbouring villages. A couple of days later, at sunset, my mother saw an animal silhouetted against the golden sky atop the hill overlooking the farm. 'The nose isn't so long and the ears aren't so sharp,' she said later. She called out, 'Karadi ... Karadi,' but it displayed none of the familiar excitement on seeing her. 'What could it be?' she asked almost afraid of what she might hear. Leopard!

When this incident occurred, we had lived in the area for a decade, and there had been no hint of a resident large predator. One elderly villager recalled the last leopard had been poisoned in the 1970s. So clearly one had moved in not long ago.

Irula tribal trackers found the spot in the garden where the dog had been killed. Following the little bits of fur caught in thorns, the trackers located the carcass in a dense, thorny thicket. I buried him under a mango tree on the farm, close to where he had been killed.

Karadi didn't know anything of the world outside the

farm, and he was certainly no match for a leopard. He wouldn't have known what got him. I felt bad I hadn't protected him enough. I was also furious with the leopard for killing my favourite dog.

For a few days, I adamantly maintained the cat had to be removed. Rom argued the leopard's case. He pointed out people lose livestock, and were able to live with these large cats with equanimity. I suspected he was thrilled to have a leopard living close by. He had said repeatedly he'd love to live amongst sabre-toothed cats, and the mere thought would send a shiver of excitement through him.

Over time, my murderous sorrow gave way to reason; the wild cat was only doing what came naturally. Call me crazy, but eventually I even began to feel possessive of the leopard. He had eaten Karadi and was therefore imbued with the dog's spirit.

We became more protective of our remaining dogs. But the cat wasn't to be dissuaded; he must have watched and timed our routine.

One early morning in March 2007, Koko, another German shepherd was attacked right in front of us when we let the dogs out after the long night. Rom, no longer sleepy-eyed, exclaimed, 'It's the bloody leopard!' Like an apparition, the cat dropped the dog and vanished. It wasn't until several minutes later that we noticed the steady drip of deep red blood from Koko's throat; her thick fur masked just how badly she was hurt.

Priya, the vet, rushed out to our farm and spent three hours stitching up the deep puncture wounds in Koko's throat, and the gashes where razor sharp claws had raked her chest and belly. While her wounds healed in time, for months afterward she coughed raspily from getting her windpipe choked.

Having a predator who called our garden 'home' was enough to send adrenalin rushing to all our senses. I imagine, from being like sluggish domestic water buffalos, we were sparked by the wild ourselves. Until then, we had taken the safety of our garden for granted; we weren't alert, listening for every single snap of twig, seeing every blade of grass move, or sniffing the air for that raunchy wild animal smell. But once the leopard arrived, our senses were as sharp as they would be in a forest. After dark, every time we stepped out of the house, we expected to see a leopard.

We knew he was around when we saw impressions of his paws pressed into soft earth after the rains. But this wasn't enough to satisfy our curiosity. We set up a camera trap to learn more about our leopard. Finally in mid-January 2009, we got a picture. The leopard was so obese that when I saw the image on the little LCD screen on the camera, I thought it was a lactating female. Later, on seeing the picture on a computer screen, we saw the obvious evidence of his manhood. I wondered if he had escaped from a zoo. Leopard researcher, Vidya Athreya, confirmed that these cats living off stray dogs and goats were indeed fat, as they didn't have to work too hard for their prey. She also cautioned that male leopards do not stick around if there are no females.

The following March, the leopard triggered the camera again. We knew it was the same chap from matching the spots. Then we lost track of him; perhaps he became camera-shy. However, we know there were leopards around; a cattle-herder witnessed one bringing down one of his calves not far from our northern fence.

People assume, as I initially did, that it was just a matter of time before a human is attacked. After all, people herding goats and cows walk these scrub forests near Chengalpattu everyday. And yet, while a few domestic animals have been lost, not a single human has been attacked even though the leopard lives in such close proximity to villages.

Our pets are no longer outdoor farm dogs; they are now house dogs. When they are outside, they are never out of our sight. The garden has become a jungle where wild b

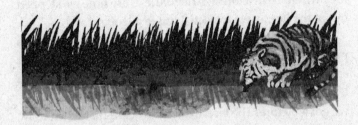

Money for Nothing

As a 13-year-old weaned on Enid Blyton and Nancy Drew stories, I demanded a weekly allowance, but my parents just brushed me away. Surreptitiously, I 'borrowed' my pocket money from my mother's purse. I didn't take much, nor did I spend it on anything. I did buy the occasional nail polish and ice cream if you must know. It gave me an immense sense of financial independence. And then one morning, in one fell swoop, I was caught, and given a lecture on 'stealing'. I became a dependent once again. But the feeling of empowerment was heady while it lasted.

Rom however, had true entrepreneurial spirit at a time when there weren't many avenues for a kid to earn a bit of spare change in India. When he was nine, living in Bombay, he and his pals filled potholes on a main road leading to an expat community on Juhu Beach. Every family contributed eight annas (50 paise), and the scheme netted him about two or three rupees over a weekend. That was a lot of money in the 1950s.

Rom even learnt the trick of making it a steady source of income by using ordinary sand. By the time the need for more pocket money arose, the sand was gone and the potholes needed filling again. No doubt, the road works department borrowed the trick from this little white kid.

Another source of income was to rid Mrs Cromby's house of sparrows. The corrugated asbestos roof sheets created gaps where they rested on the beam, and this was where sparrows roosted. The birds are really messy, and when there are too many of them, the house begins to smell like a poultry farm. Mrs Cromby offered four annas (25 paise) for every sparrow caught. After dark, Rom climbed up a stepladder and by blocking both sides of the gap, trapped the sparrows. In all, he recalls catching about nine sparrows and earning two rupees and four annas. In those days, no one ever thought that this plentiful bird would disappear, or that nearly 60 years hence that a World House Sparrow Day would be declared.

Boarding school did nothing to hinder Rom's enterprising skills. Although he had learnt to fish for mirror carp in the Kodaikanal Lake from local fishermen, he didn't relish eating the mushy-textured fish. But he noticed that others loved it, and he put up a notice on the school bulletin board which went something like this: 'You can buy fish on order, just tell me on Friday.' The going rate was five rupees per kilo, and several of the school staff placed orders. Instead of going to Sunday School, Rom spent his weekends on the lake, doing what he liked best – fishing.

Adults these days were the kids of my time, and clearly, are made of quite different stuff. According to a Cartoon Network survey of 2009, urban Indian kids were expected to 'earn' as much as Rs 664 crores as pocket money that year, compared to Rs 478 crores in 2008. Some children of Ludhiana made out like bandits, receiving as much as

Rs 1,600 per week. The same survey also showed that children didn't splurge; instead 62 per cent of them saved some of the cash at least. Clearly some kids are also learning a few good lessons not just in financial management, but frugality and thrift along the way.

I tried to imagine whether I could have earned pocket money as Rom had. No one in my family or neighbourhood would think of giving kids money in exchange for labour. Help was always to be provided free, whether it was babysitting my brother or other kids in the neighbourhood, preparing vegetables for cooking, running errands, or cleaning up the house. It was my 'duty', I was told. If my parents had thrown in some money with 'duty', I would have done double the work with alacrity.

Danger in Paradise

White sands, turquoise blue seas, lush greenery – it is everyone's dream holiday destination. It isn't just the South Pacific or the Caribbean that boast of these idyllic islands; there is India's own Havelock Island of the Andamans.

It was late evening on 28 April 2010, when Rom received a frantic call from Havelock. An Indian-American tourist, Jito Chadha had gone snorkelling with his girlfriend, Lauren, that afternoon. He said he was underwater filming a moray eel at Neil's Cove, when he heard Lauren scream. He looked up to see her head in the jaws of a large saltwater crocodile (saltie). Jito said he dropped his camera, and grabbed the croc by the tail, hoping to rescue Lauren. When the beast didn't let his girlfriend go, he tried to pry the animal's jaws open to no avail. When Jito surfaced to breathe, the saltie carried the girl away by swimming along the bottom of the sea.

Crocs are known to swim away with their prey on the surface of the water, not carry them underwater. Besides, Neil's Cove is along Beach No. 7, the most popular beach in the Andamans, and nobody had ever seen a crocodile there before. The closest known population of these reptiles was across the sea at Baratang in Middle Straits, 14 kms to the west. There were no mangroves in the vicinity of the incident, and salties are not known to brazenly attack in open waters. The more we thought about it, the more improbable the story seemed.

Samit, who runs the resort, wanted to know if the story was plausible. Highly unlikely, replied Rom, and Australian saltie experts whom Rom consulted echoed that prognosis. Nobody in Havelock believed Jito's tale. But where was the girl? There was no sign of the camera, snorkelling gear, flippers, nothing. The resort launched a massive manhunt with divers combing the area for clues.

Luckily for Jito, almost 48 hours later, they found the camera resting on the sea floor. Another stroke of luck – just 20 seconds prior to the attack, the young man had switched on the camera's video function. As it sank to the bottom of the sea, it recorded snatches of the terrible action playing out near the surface. And it clearly showed the sequence of events that Jito had been repeating for the previous two days.

Soon after, a search party found both the croc and the body of the girl about three kms away. Beaches in Havelock were closed to the public, and Operation Catch-the-Saltie was launched. Over a month later, in the early hours of 1 June, the four-metre-long croc was trapped nine kms from the site of the fatal attack. By the end of the day, it was moved to Haddo Zoo in Port Blair.

How did a saltie brave the open ocean to get to Havelock in the first place? During the 1600s, now-extinct crocs were found in distant Seychelles. The reptiles were thought to be Nile crocodiles because of the islands' proximity to Africa.

However, scientists who've examined the preserved skulls say that salties ruled the roost here, about 2,700 kms away from the closest population in Sri Lanka. Over the years, salties have shown up in such far-flung oceanic islands as the Maldives and the Ryukyu islands of Japan, while breeding populations exist on several islands of Micronesia and Melanesia in the Pacific Ocean.

Research shows that surface currents make salties accomplished ocean-farers. Some are known to plan their journeys, and if the currents are unfavourable, will wait on shore until the tide changes. However, we'll never know the swim path of the Havelock croc.

We learnt some new lessons in saltie behaviour from this episode. Salties can carry away prey underwater under certain circumstances. Perhaps this was the croc's way of making a quick getaway, because Jito was harassing it. We also learnt not to be complacent in open beaches, especially when there was a population of crocs nearby. What's 14 kms when the species is capable of navigating 2,000 kms in the open ocean?

Pogeyan Puli: The Smokey Cat

If we'd heard the story of this unusual animal from someone else, we would have dismissed it right away. Rom has known Santosh Mani, a tea estate manager in Munnar, Kerala, for nearly 40 years. We paid attention when Santosh said that he saw the creature twice over a period of five years at the same spot. It was a cat, almost as big as a leopard with a long tail, but it had no spots. It was crossing the road from one tea field to another, so Santosh was able to get a good look.

I suggested that perhaps Santosh had seen a leopard after dark. Dull light creates an optical illusion; the leopard's spots seem to disappear making the animal look more like an American mountain lion. Santosh however, said he had seen the creature in the early afternoon. He made enquiries with the local tribals, the Mudhuvan, and of course, they knew about it. They called it the 'pogeyan puli', 'smokey cat', and clearly distinguished it from the leopard, tiger and jungle cat.

A few weeks later, we ran into another friend, James Zacharia, a Kerala Forest Department official who had also seen the pogeyan. James was climbing up a steep slope in Eravikulam National Park. Pausing to catch his breath, he had looked up to find himself staring straight into the eyes of Ole Smokey. The cat was lying on a rocky ledge looking down at him. Then quietly it vanished like only cats can do.

Rom wrote to various institutions and cat experts urging them to investigate the creature, but there was no response and we left it at that.

Then Sandesh Kadur, a wildlife filmmaker, said he had seen one at Eravikulam too. It was daylight, and he had watched the cat walking calmly across the grassland.

'Why didn't you get a picture?' I demanded.

'I was afraid that it might run away if I moved. So I just stood still, memorizing every feature of the pogeyan,' he replied.

At that time, Sandesh hadn't heard of the pogeyan. He described it as a 'jungle cat on steroids' and asked others what it was.

A few years later, he was commissioned by the BBC to make a film about the cat. He set up camera traps hoping to get the evidence that he had so narrowly missed last time. More than 200 camera trap-nights later, there was no image of the cat.

Since we hadn't been able to help him solve the identity of the mysterious cat, Santosh sought out interested people in cryptozoology circles. One evening I got a call from him and he said excitedly, 'I found it! It's the Asiatic golden cat!' My jaw dropped. The golden cat is found only in Southeast Asia and nowhere on peninsular India. When I looked it up in our mammal book, I had to admit that it matched Santosh's description of the pogeyan. I stuttered, 'B-b-but, that's impossible!' Santosh wasn't listening. After years of his story falling on deaf ears, he had finally found an explanation, a closure.

In the meantime, Sandesh thought the animal he may have seen was a large jungle cat. He said, 'Illustrations in books don't do justice to the length of the jungle cat's tail. It is not as short as a bobcat's, but quite a bit longer. If it is not a jungle cat, what else could it be?'

Perhaps, like some other animals, jungle cats grow larger in cool, higher elevations. Santosh however, wasn't buying it. Sandesh may have seen a jungle cat, but the animal he saw, he swore, was much larger than any jungle cat but smaller than a leopard. Besides, the Mudhuvan also know the difference between the jungle cat and pogeyan puli.

Just as the black leopard is a result of genetic mutation, is it possible the pogeyan is a spotless mutation? Or, is the pogeyan, indeed, a relict population of the golden cat? The issue is so muddled, we'll need more than a photograph to identify the cat.

I asked Mohan Alembath, a former forest department official and a keen wildlife observer, if he had any insights. He sent me a link to a YouTube video featuring an Asiatic golden cat taken in Indonesia and said, 'The golden cat shown in this video looks exactly like the pogeyan.' He went further, 'I have seen pogeyan only once, but it was at very close quarters. I was coming back from Poovar and I was rounding a bend in the road.  The cat was smack in front of me, barely 50 metres away. There is no mistaking it for anything else. Until I saw him, I had believed the Muduvan were spinning a yarn. I am 100 per cent sure that Smokey exists.'

Feckless Farmers

If you live on a farm, there is definite peer pressure to grow something. 'Do you have a kitchen garden?' is the commonest question visitors ask. Initially, it was the proverbial first-time farmer's luck; we had a glut of everything – more tomatoes, lettuce, spinach, basil, fennel and gourds than we knew what to do with. It became necessary to make more friends just to give away our surplus veggies; we had become successful organic farmers.

Our farm, formerly a rice-field, is squarely sandwiched between scrub jungle and farmland. As conservationists are wont to do, we planted lots of trees. We were desperate for the shade, and besides, all Rom can think of doing with even the tiniest parcel of land is to plant saplings. Our architect was apoplectic when Rom put a tree right next to the house instead of maintaining the mandatory 15 feet distance. By that, I mean, close enough that the trunk rubs against the roof and leans heavily on the house during a storm.

Then, after 12 years, the trees had grown, the farm integrated with the jungle, and there was no clear boundary. Animals started wandering onto the property, and like a typical human, I began muttering, 'Can't they see the fence? Why don't they stay in the forest?'

Trees provided the bridge for several troops of bonnet monkeys to go from forest to fields, but not without first tasting our produce. Palm squirrels used the trees as a launch pad for their guerilla warfare on the kitchen garden. Half-eaten green tomatoes, guavas and mangoes littered the ground, while tender, green, badly mauled chardonnay melons hung from vines. Presumably, the squirrels and monkeys decided to solve our problem of producing too much.

No matter what we planted, pests, large and small, worked even more diligently than us. One season, monkeys and jackals ran through our crop of peanuts, and what was left cost us Rs 500 a kilogramme to grow. But our worst enemies were the monkeys, celebrated across the country as the earthly avatar of Hanuman, the monkey god.

Initially our dogs were effective guardians of the garden, but the primates rapidly learned that dogs don't climb trees. So we brought out the catapults. But the monkeys were already savvy enough to sit tightly out of reach of the stones. Once our backs were turned, they were again raiding. To get ahead in this game, we would have to drop everything and watch the garden full time. Like other farmers, we were tempted to resort to the 'atom bomb' fire crackers, but the sound drives the dogs crazy.

When the maths didn't tally, we thumbed our noses at the pests by giving up farming altogether. You could say it was a case of sour peanuts. Our neighbours in the village just looked at each other and tapped their temples, the universal sign language for having a screw loose. Now the only things that survive the hordes are spinach and limes.

We are not the only ones singled out by monkeys. Across India, several villages are plagued by them. Recently Dr Mewa Singh and his students from the University of Mysore reported that throughout Karnataka, these monkeys have been virtually wiped out of the coastal region. In some districts such as Chitradurga, temples and tourist spots, teeming with these primates 20 years ago, now have none. What is happening in other states is anybody's guess. Who would have thought that a creature sanctified by religion may likely need conservation action one day?

At least we had the luxury of giving up farming since we made a living in other ways. Many farmers across India who rely on the produce of their land have no choice but to brave the monkeys' raids. On the farm, we keep the primates on their toes just so they don't have designs on our house. We have already proved ourselves to be wimps once.

Croc Whisperer

Many years ago, I pointed to pictures of Thai crocodile and American alligator wrestlers with their heads inside gaping toothy jaws, and incredulously asked Rom, 'Surely those animals are trained, aren't they?' Rom thought the trainers just intimidated the animals enough so they wouldn't bite during the show. The accepted wisdom then was crocs can be tamed but not trained.

In Irian Jaya, Indonesia, Rom had seen a five-foot-long New Guinea freshwater croc that lived in a wooden house on stilts. It had grown up alongside children, people and dogs from the time it was a mere hatchling. On cool rainy nights, it lay by the fire warming itself along with the community members.

Ralf Sommerlad, the director of the Madras Crocodile Bank briefly in mid-2008, recalled seeing a man with his pet caiman, a kind of South American crocodile, in Frankfurt. When the man knelt down, the caiman would rub against his head and shoulders much like a puppy wanting to be petted. Ralf initiated a programme to start training the reptiles at the Madras Crocodile Bank. Soham Mukherjee, the assistant curator, developed the idea into an increasingly fun and fascinating programme for both people and crocs. He began with a young six-year-old American alligator, Ally.

Ally had been handled as a baby, but since she had grown, the practice had been abandoned. She still remembered her name, a good starting point. Every time she obeyed a command, she was rewarded with a little piece of meat. It was no different than training a dog, albeit a long, scaly one.

A week later, while training Ally, Soham noticed a mugger in the background correctly responding to his commands. The croc had been watching and learning without the aid of any treats. Pintu promptly joined the programme too. Soon, a motley assortment of crocs of different species, such as Komodo and Thai – the Siamese crocs, Mick – the saltwater croc, and Abu – the Nile croc, were attending the Croc School.

Training began everyday at 3:00 p.m. About 10 minutes ahead of time, the six pupils waited with anticipation at the edge of the pool, alert to the faintest sound of Soham's voice. Once he arrived, their excitement was palpable. The croc students knew in which order they would be called, and awaited their turn patiently. And they were just like my dogs, knowing the sequence of commands so well that they preempted Soham. So the commands had to be in a different order every time. The crocodilian pupils even learned when Soham's weekly day off fell.

Eventually, even older animals such as Rambo, an adult mugger, joined the programme, and demonstrated that age is no barrier to learning new tricks. But the spoilt favourite, Ally, is the star pupil who knows 12 commands like 'come', 'water', 'stay', 'up', 'sit', 'turn', 'open your mouth'.

Once when Ally was half way up the training ramp, Soham asked her to 'jump'. As can be imagined, it is difficult to jump on an incline, but neither did she want to pass up the chance of earning a treat. So she raised herself on her toes and lay down flat on her stomach, miming a slow-motion jump without leaving the ground. Pretty amazing when you consider that Ally's brain is about the size of a walnut.

Today, 30 crocodiles of 11 different species from 8-months-young to 40-years-old are in various stages of training. Pupils now include caiman lizards and Aldabra tortoises, and the school has been renamed Reptile School. Snakes, monitor lizards and turtles are on the waiting list, and apparently, in strict adherence to government regulations, there is no capitation fee for admission.

The Drug Runner

In the early 1970s, the Madras Snake Park was the regular
hangout for a variety of Western hippies, students from
nearby colleges, and animal-crazy kids from the city. One
fixture for a few months in 1972 was a man who had
introduced himself as Nat Finkelstein, an animal dealer.
After some time, he admitted that he was facing drug
smuggling charges. Rom remembered reading the
newspaper reports several months earlier.

Nat had been trying to send two sloth bear cubs to
California when the Madras Customs was tipped off that he
was actually smuggling drugs. They confiscated the
shipment at the airport, shoved the young bears into the
records room, and tore the wooden cage apart looking for
the contraband. Cakes of hashish encased in polyurethane
were stuffed within the walls and floor boards.

Meanwhile, the scared and frustrated bears went to work
like a maelstrom, ripping, shitting, and chewing on every
file in the room. Although I had heard this story several
times, I never failed to laugh with glee. How often had I
daydreamt of revenge on the obdurate bureaucracy!

Nat spent nine months in jail before getting out on bail,

and this was when he started visiting the Snake Park, much to Rom's discomfort. 'In the middle of the public area, Nat would roll up these huge hashish cigars, and there was nothing I could do to dissuade him,' Rom complained. And then, one fine day, just as suddenly as he had appeared, Nat jumped bail and vanished, never to be seen again. Even now, decades later, Rom's relief is palpable.

When Rom narrated Nat's story for the first time, I was intrigued. 'Tell me more, tell me more,' I had begged, ever the story-junkie. Rom said Nat lived in an air-conditioned apartment as his pet, a huge Tibetan mastiff, 'Face', couldn't tolerate Madras weather. Face was immensely protective of Nat and Jill's child, and wouldn't let any strangers approach. Rom had no more details to add.

One night, as I sat uninspired at the computer, trying to write, I remembered Nat and his paper-destroying bears. Curious to know where this character had washed up, I googled him just for distraction. There were several pages of links to a well-known celebrity photographer. But Rom said the Nat he knew wasn't a photographer, never carried a camera. There was no one else of the same name; it was as if *the* Nat Finkelstein had vanished into thin air like Rumpelstiltskin. I tried googling 'animal dealer', 'hashish smuggler', 'India'. Nothing. Blank.

Thoroughly distracted, I started reading about the photographer, Nat Finkelstein. He had been Andy Warhol's 'court photographer' for three years, and his images of the artist and his groupies were arresting. The picture that really caught my attention was one of Andy standing with Bob Dylan in profile with a silk screen portrait print of Elvis Presley in the background – an iconic image of the biggest icons of pop and counter-culture of the 1960s. Other photographs included the rock-band – The Velvet Underground, the artists Marcel Duchamp and Salvador Dali, and the poet Allen Ginsberg.

And then, a quote caught my eye: 'I used to sell Ella Fitzgerald and Errol Garner weed.' Could this be the Nat Finkelstein I was hunting for? Rom drawled, 'Naaaa. None of this adds up. If he was a photographer, he would have told me. He knew I listened to Bob Dylan a lot . . . no . . . you're wasting your time.'

I shuffled through the web pages again and found a picture of the photographer.

'Is this him?' I asked, dragging Rom back from the movie he was watching.

'He's too old. Show me one of him about 30 years younger.'

I strummed the web again like a spider checking if her prey had been caught. Photographers spend their lifetimes taking other people's pictures, and are rarely photographed themselves. I wasn't getting anywhere, and perhaps, I was just wasting my time. But I was hooked and continued searching.

Besides the art world, the photographer Nat was also closely associated with the Black Panthers, going to the extent of procuring arms for them. In 1969, he began to fear that the US government was after his life, and when an arrest warrant was issued on an old drug charge, he fled the country. Excitedly I scanned down to see if he went to India. He followed the Silk Route into the Middle East and . . . sold hashish to earn a living. Two Nat Finkelsteins selling dope from the same neighbourhood? But there was no clinching evidence that they were one and the same.

One site said that Nat, the photographer came as far as Kathmandu.

'That's close, isn't it?' I interrupted Rom's movie again.

'Yeah, he said he sent some special breed of horse from Nepal to the US.'

The search was getting warm, but I wanted red heat. On Nat's website, I found pictures of his Tibetan mastiff, 'Goochie'. Was it a coincidence that both Nats appeared to like Tibetan mastiffs?

Nat Finkelstein returned to the US in 1982, when he learnt that charges against him had been dropped. There was no other information on what he did in those intervening dozen years abroad. After his return, Nat managed a punk noise band called Khmer Rouge, and photo-chronicled the younger subcultures of New York. He also became addicted to cocaine, and flew to Bolivia to feed his habit. When Andy Warhol died in 1987, a shocked Nat cleaned up his act. He went back to photography, and today his pictures appear in several major collections around the world. He died in 2009, survived by his wife, Elizabeth and a brother. There was no mention of Jill or their son. In fact, one site even said he had no children. Dead end.

I went around in circles, spinning a wider web, adding more search words, using different combinations. A local New York paper reported that in 2005, Nat and his dog, another Tibetan mastiff called 'Bling', fell into a sewer because the manhole cover was askew. Insignificant trivia but one of the readers commented that Nat was married to a 30-year-old woman. Could Jill have been an earlier wife? I started a new search for Nat's wives, despite protests from several parts of my brain that I was stepping beyond the limits of privacy. There had been five of them and Elizabeth was the last.

It was getting close to my bedtime, and although there were some tantalizing similarities, the worlds of Nat Finkelstein, the animal trader and Nat Finkelstein, the photographer seemed poles apart. There was just one last page to check before I decided to call it quits.

Uncomfortably, I scrolled down Nat's reminiscences of the wild 60s – parties, drugs, sex, and bitchy celebrity politics. Right at the very end was the name I was looking for, and I slammed the desk in vindication. Rom jumped and looked perplexedly at my triumphant face. I pointed to the screen where photographer Nat Finkelstein said he was married to Jill. That was it, the only nail to hold the two disparate lives together as a whole. Nat Finkelstein, the drug smuggling animal trader *was* Nat Finkelstein, the photographer of the New York *avant garde*. Poor Rom was strangely quiet for once and mumbled, 'But he never said anything to me.'

Several hours later, I found a piece written by Nat where he mentioned Jill and their child, and I knew beyond a shred of doubt that I had found my man. But nowhere in the chronicles online was there any mention of Nat, the animal trader. Did he exist only in Rom's tale?

I sought Nina's help. Rom's sister had helped him start the Snake Park. Did she remember anything more of Nat's animal trading? I asked. She managed to track down a book titled *King of Nepal* by Joseph Pietri.

In 1969, almost immediately after fleeing from the US, Nat had set himself up in Nepal and entered into a deal with a rising rock 'n' roll musician, Peter Kelly. The former would ship Tibetan mastiffs in wooden crates stuffed with the finest hashish to the latter. These dogs are of dramatic size, weight and colour, and were virtually unknown in the US. So although the customs officials at JFK airport showed a great deal of interest in the shipment, and the drug sniffing dogs were excited by the bear-like animal, they failed to detect the contraband right under their noses. It was idiot-proof, author Pietri gloated. Focusing more on his music career, Kelly sent his sidekick, Pietri to Nepal to pay Nat his share of the booty.

At that time, Nat was scouring the countryside for another Nepali speciality, a unique Tibetan pony. Pietri says they eventually found a mean-tempered freak whose head was larger than his body. This was the 'special horse' Rom remembered. Nat accompanied the pony overland to Bombay, where it was to be put on a flight to the US; Pietri had been left behind in Nepal. Bad move.

In Nat's absence, Pietri cut his own deal with the former's Nepali partner, a local lama, and took over the business. Nat was not only left out in the cold but was also never to enter Nepal again.

Pietri writes his goal was to 'put a Tibetan mastiff in every major American city', which he almost accomplished. Most of these dogs found in the US today are apparently descendants of the early drug-runners.

After several shipments, Pietri began running out of dogs, and one of the last he sent didn't take kindly to being cooped up. It managed to bite through the crate, and escape into the plane's cargo hold by the time the flight landed in London. The Royal Society for the Prevention of Cruelty to Animals put the dog into one of their own cages, and sent it onward to the US. The scam was revealed when the mangled crate was burnt, and the heady hash fumes threatened to intoxicate all present. But since the dog had been sent from India, and investigations didn't lead to the kingpins in Nepal, there were no arrests.

Pietri then sent red pandas and a young rhino to the US successfully. In the meantime, Nat had moved to Madras, and decided to get back into the business. He procured two sloth bear cubs, Dora and Flora, in whose crate he embedded 15 kgs of hashish and was caught red-handed. It appears to have been his only attempt at trading in wild animals.

Pietri indicates that Nat's obnoxious personality probably did him in. However, reading these excerpts from the book jogged Rom's memory. He remembered Nat suspected Todd, one of Pietri's accomplices, for having ratted on him.

In the meantime, Pietri had been planning to send a shipment of two Himalayan black bears, and despite the fiasco in Madras, his contacts in the US insisted he go ahead with the deal. When the bears arrived, the now-suspicious US authorities drilled holes in the cages, and found the contraband. One crate is still on display at the US Customs Museum in San Francisco.

Perhaps Nat didn't want anyone in Madras to know the true nature of his business and therefore didn't brag about his celebrity connections. Whatever his reasons, Rom and Nina remain astonished by the colourful and unsavoury history of a character they once knew briefly.

Croc Bank Ants

The ants came from Guindy, a neighbourhood in Chennai where the Madras Snake Park is located. Rom remembered that in the mid-1980s, he had moved an old, decrepit refrigerator from the Snake Park to the Croc Bank, and when it was unloaded, a whole lot of ants spilt out. Nobody thought twice about it then. Almost a decade later, these ants suddenly reared their ugly red heads by the tens of thousands.

At night, they marched in military order; if they were not scouting for sugar, nectar, anything sweet, they were looking for a place to nest. If they moved into the closet while we were away, the clothes developed damp, yellowish, indelible spots. During the evenings, there were so many on the floor that everyone sat cross-legged on chairs and tables.

One morning, I even found them inside the computer's CPU. Hurriedly, I undid the screws of the cover, ran outside the office, and maniacally shook it free of ants, larva and eggs. Rom was worried that all that shaking would loosen a circuit board or two, but I was too hysterical to take any notice of his concerns. There was only one good thing about these ants from hell – they didn't bite.

Sleep was possible only under mosquito nets. In the middle of the night, lines of ants walked along the net stays and sides. We teased our guests, 'Hope we don't see you being carried away by ants!' They smiled nervously in response. After a while the jokes got stale, and we could take it no longer. *War!*

Crews were sent out into the grounds to hunt and destroy. The no-chemical policy was temporarily rescinded and noxious insecticides purchased. Starting from one end, the ant exterminators worked their way up the Croc Bank campus. The nests, located at the base of trees, had to be dug up, and then the whole lot sprayed with poison. Even as this enterprise was partly underway, fresh ant nests were discovered in the newly cleared area. It was a decidedly losing battle; we were outnumbered and out-manoeuvred.

We figured that keeping houses and offices clean of ants was more practical than ridding the entire property of the pests. We threw sheaves of tobacco leaves with abandon into library bookshelves, clothes closets, and kitchen cupboards. Our clothes may have smelt a bit strange, but nobody commented. Plants touching the buildings were pruned and overhead cables buried. The security staff on night-duty was primed to keep an eye out for ant invaders.

We set out little dishes of sweetened boric acid liquid every night. Worker ants would carry the poison back to the nest and kill the queen and nest-mates. At several kilogrammes of sugar a week, it wasn't cheap. When one nest died, another moved in. For months it seemed like we were hardly making any headway. None of the experts we contacted could comprehend the scale of our problem, and dinner-time conversation sounded like a war-room meeting.

And then suddenly there was a remarkable change; the ants virtually disappeared. The answer to our prayers? Toads. Little ones, medium ones, and huge fat mammas were everywhere. At every step, several toads jumped out of the way. Each would position itself along a line of ants, and methodically tongue them up like picking prey off a conveyor belt. During our after-dinner walks, we came upon big toads so stuffed that they couldn't hop anymore. With their stomachs grossly distended, all they could manage was a waddle 'n' roll. Relief made us laugh with just an edge of hysteria at these toad antics.

Within the next couple of years, the ant problem all but ceased to exist, and there was peace. Then we moved to our farm near Chengalpattu, and one night, a few years later, we stared in utter horror as hundreds of the distinctive Croc Bank ants marched into the house. We could almost hear the drumbeats of war in the distance.

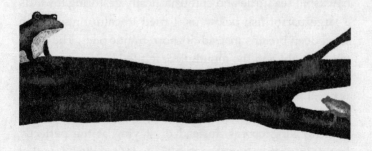

Off the Deep End

About two decades ago, I learnt to snorkel in a hotel swimming pool. Weeks later, I followed Rom's example and, clutching my mask over my face, leapt off a pier in the Andamans. I was used to the visible depth of the pool, but here water stretched into infinite blackness. Fear and vertigo gripped my throat like a vise.

Rom was of course tripping out – swimming alongside a hawksbill sea turtle and enthusiastically gesturing towards a large parrot fish below us. I tried to calm myself with long, deep breaths instead of short, frantic ones. The mask felt too tight and the mouthpiece felt too big; it wasn't fun or comfortable. In a strange reversal, I felt like a fish out of water. I lasted a few minutes more and then I was out.

Another time, Rom and I went to Agumbe, Karnataka, to look for king cobras. Instead of staying at the perfectly livable inspection bungalow for 25 rupees a night, he wanted to camp in the forest. It was pouring rain.

'Who in his right mind would camp in such weather?' I demanded.

He said, 'I want to be in the middle of the jungle. I don't want to commute from the village.'

We pitched our tent in a small clearing deep inside the dark jungle. Although there was hardly any dry firewood, we managed to boil some water for instant noodles. As we stood in the rain under umbrellas slurping up our frugal dinner, legions of leeches inched towards us. Nothing had prepared me for this – the extreme leech experience. The whole forest floor seemed to be alive and seething with eager little rubbery vampires.

We wore Christmas stocking-like 'leech socks'. Since leeches can get through knitted socks, these special socks are made of woven cloth. They are worn over regular socks, and fastened at the knees with elastic or string. Insecticide is sprayed over the whole leg to dissuade the blood-suckers from climbing up. During the rains, the chemical can be washed into a pristine habitat, so we go easy on the spray. Instead, we spend most of our time flicking leeches off as we did during those few days in Agumbe.

The only respite from the bloodsuckers came that night, when we were zipped up in the tent. During the day, it drizzled constantly, and there was no sun. The humidity was so high that clothes, sleeping bags, everything was damp. Our treks in the forest didn't lift my spirits either. The tall forest seemed darkly foreboding and claustrophobic. We didn't see any animals; they were all sensibly tucked away from the rain, I suspected. I yearned for the sun, heat, and open sky. Two days of mucking about in the rain with hardly any food, except instant *bleep* noodles three times a day, gnawed at my energy and soul. What did king cobras do in the rains? Was it business as usual, or did they hunker down and wait for the season to pass? At that moment, I didn't care what they did. I wanted out *now*; after all, I was a dyed-in-the-wool city slicker not so long ago.

Despondently, Rom agreed to break camp and live in the village. Could he really be having fun in this mess, I wondered. Could she really want to leave this magical place, he wondered. At least, nights were comfortable in the inspection bungalow, even if mucking about in the forest during the rain was no fun.

Rom appeared to have a habit of throwing me off the deep end. But on reflection, it was probably a good thing. Every subsequent trip to the jungle was compared to that first one to Agumbe and nothing really fazed me after that.

A few years later, I was on a trip to Namdapha in remote Arunachal Pradesh with a group of people who had never been in a rainforest before. The monsoon showed no signs of abating, everything was damp, leeches were out with a vengeance, and my fellow travellers were as miserable as I had been on my first rainforest camping trip. But this camp had a crucial difference. We had a cook and valet who laid out three-course meals thrice a day. While the others were fretting about the inconveniences of the jungle, I was stuffed with good food, and watching hoolock gibbons, flying squirrels, martens and other creatures.

How was this transformation possible? I had realized along the way that saying 'yes' to every opportunity was like opening a door to a possibility – adventure. I learned that when I jumped all the way in, I was accepting the wild, untamed reality Rom loved so much. I also learned that there was always plenty of time later to wallow in one's comfort zone, but this moment, when an option presents itself, may never come again . . . so grab it.

Creature Comforts

When I was growing up, I wanted a dog for a pet. Unfortunately my parents ruled we weren't going to have one. So it fell under the long checklist called 'When I grow up . . .'

One of the things I asked Rom when we first met was what pets he had had when he was young. He was in a different league altogether – a fruit bat, black kites, rose-ringed parakeets, drongos, mongooses, civet cats, a fox, a jungle cat, tarantulas, a macaw, monitor lizards, a jungle crow, a gila monster, various snakes of course, and many others. I followed that up with an endless stream of questions – what did the animals eat, how they played, what they were like. He perhaps felt he had made a mistake admitting that he had owned these creatures at all.

By far, his favourite pet was an Indian python which lived under his bed in the school dorm for about four years. On cold mornings in Kodaikanal, Tamil Nadu, Rom remembered basking in the sun with his pet and some of his friends. If anyone else came by, Rom casually flung a cloth over the snake, and surprisingly no one in school found out.

During vacations, the python would travel back to Bombay

with him. When Rom's grandma – Amma Doodles – didn't feel like meeting guests, she'd invite them cheerily, 'My grandson has come home on vacation with his pet python. You must meet them both!' Surprisingly, they usually had somewhere else to go that they just happened to remember. A few, however, were intrigued and couldn't be put off. Rom would then have to bring the sleek snake out.

Once, when Rom was about 16, the snake got loose at the apartment in Bombay and couldn't be found anywhere. He searched high and low, in every room and cupboard. Nothing. How was he to tell the others on the block without causing pandemonium? Rom came up with a plan with the help of his mother. He knocked on every door in the building, introduced himself, and asked, 'I've lost a pet. Have you noticed anything unusual?'

Usually people just retorted, 'No.'

However, some asked, 'What pet?'

Rom replied in a mumble, 'It's a very friendly ... cuddly ... loveable ... python. Very small. Just eight feet long.'

Nobody had seen it.

10 to 15 days went by with no news. The apartment building overlooked a steep slope covered in jungle. Peacocks woke everyone up at 4 a.m., and there were cobras, ratsnakes, birds of many kinds, and large bandicoots. Rom figured the snake could live out its life in this forest without a problem.

Then one day, Amma Doodles had to make a trip to Delhi, and Rom went up into the storeroom to get the suitcases. He moved a whole pile of trunks and in the six inch gap made by the wooden slats, lo and behold! There was the fat python coiled up neatly. It had somehow managed to jam itself into the tiny space. It was going to shed its skin, and at this time snakes seek a quiet place. In its newfound freedom, the python had just gone from one room to another when it could have gone anywhere.

A year later, before he left for the States ostensibly for higher education, Rom gave his pet away to a friend.

Subsequently I had my fill of pets too – baby pythons, sand boas, star tortoises, and crocodiles. Some arrived at my door unbidden as orphans – mongooses, toddy cats, a hare, a koel, and they all left when they became adults. But once we moved to the farm, I got a dog, actually several dogs, and I finally fulfilled my childhood dream.

The Great Brain Robbery

Toxoplasma is a science non-fiction nightmare. Closely related to the malaria-causing protozoan, it reproduces in cats' guts, and eggs are shed in feline feces. Rats nibble on the poop and get infected. After living inside a rodent, when it comes time to reproduce, the parasite has to make the leap into a cat's gut again.

Rats are pathologically averse to cats; the mere smell of one is enough to drive them away. How does toxo jump from prey to predator? The parasite severs particular neurons in the rat's brain, without touching any of the other functions, making it fearless of cats. A neurosurgeon *par excellence*!

The parasite goes even further, fiddling with a neural pathway in the brain so the smell of cats becomes sexually alluring. The poor rodent throws caution to the winds and flaunts itself. *Hara-kiri*! Toxo hits jackpot and can now merrily reproduce. But this is only one of the world's parasitical neurosurgeons.

Have you heard of hairworms? The thin-as-a-strand-of-hair worm grows inside grasshoppers, and after it matures, it doesn't take the easy way out through the cloaca. Instead it messes with the grasshopper's brain leading it to commit suicide. The poor insect leaps headlong into a puddle of water with all the confidence of an expert swimmer only to drown. Once its host is dead, the hairworm wriggles free to reproduce in water.

Then there is a barnacle, sacculina that rides piggyback on crabs. When it comes time to lay eggs, the barnacle needs a hole in the sand. Since sacculina is incapable of movement, how does it do that? First, it renders the crab impotent so the latter nurtures the parasite's eggs as its own. Then the barnacle controls the crab to do its bidding and digging. Voila!

However, what sets the rat-cat parasite, toxo, in a class apart is not only its widespread prevalence, but its wicked effects on humans. Most people do not get infected by cats directly, but by eating uncooked meat, drinking unsafe water, gardening without wearing gloves, or walking barefoot. A few years ago, suspected contamination of the municipal water supply led to an outbreak of toxo in Coimbatore, Tamil Nadu.

Globally, as much as a third (maybe more) of the human population is estimated to be infected with the disease. In India, 45 per cent of pregnant women test positive every year. Unlike H1N1, toxo is not front page news because it is not believed to be fatal to healthy humans, nor is it infectious. But if you are a baby or your immunity is lowered by drugs or disease, then toxo can take your life.

What toxo does to healthy humans is alter their personalities. Infected men become morose, jealous, and introverted with high levels of testosterone, while it makes women outgoing, animated, and warm. As Dr Nicky Boulter of the Sydney University of Technology puts it, 'It can make men behave like alley cats and women like sex kittens.'

The sting at the end of the toxo tale is – it makes both men and women reckless and uninhibited. Toxo-muddled human beings are three times more likely to be involved in road accidents than others. So next time you see yet another suicidal person on the road and grumble, 'What's with them?' you now know.

When a human personality-altering disease like toxo is widespread, its effects across a country's population can be startling. Countries with high infection rates show high rates of neuroses. It could be one of the main factors manipulating human culture itself, believe scientists.

As I muse about the wickedness of toxo, a startling thought occurs to me – humans may not be a dead end for the parasite. Is it possible infected people may be falling prey to wild tigers and leopards in our forests and farmlands? Are the testosterone-driven men across the world who free-handle venomous snakes at risk to their lives infected too? Perhaps even suicide bombers? These are just the musings of my hyperactive and possibly parasite-enslaved brain, but I wouldn't be surprised if they were proved true.

Close Encounters

What should people be wary of while walking in the jungles of India? No, not tigers and leopards, or even leeches. But elephants and sloth bears!

When I first went on treks into the jungle with Rom, he taught me to be aware of wind direction (you want to be downwind of an elephant so you can smell it first), sounds of snapping branches and rumbling elephant bellies, any snorting and blowing (a sloth bear busy with a termite mound). He also taught me to identify escape routes should we get up-close to an elephant. It was nerve-wracking initially, but eventually it became second nature.

Should you sense an elephant or bear, you quietly melt away into the forest in the opposite direction. But if your senses fail you and you come face to face with an elephant, what do you do? Climb a tree, run downhill or across boulders; use the topography in your favour. On level ground, zigzag across the forest, never run in a straight line, as surprisingly, elephants can outrun you.

When a bear is engrossed in hoovering up termites, he's not listening very well. If it is too late to retreat without being noticed, call attention to yourself – cough or whistle just loud enough to alert it. It can be a fine balance between protecting life and limb, and enjoying the pleasures of the wild.

Should you startle a sloth bear, there is little chance that it will run away. It lashes out with its long earth-ripping claws, with terrible consequences.

Rom had three close encounters with bears, and thankfully he was able to duck behind a bush or tree every time. Many people have not been as fortunate, and have had their faces torn, heads scalped or even been killed. The price for not being aware in the jungle is quite high. Usually I carry a stick which in a pinch could distract a charging bear, but thankfully I've never had a chance to try it out.

Rom recalls that Kenneth Anderson's son, Don, shared his bed with a pet sloth bear. Until the shaggy animal woke up of his own accord (late in the morning), Don just could not afford to move.

Some individual animals can be cantankerous, and don't abide by these broad generalizations. A few years ago, a few friends were trekking through a forest. One of them went for a stroll along a dry river bed. When she saw a sloth bear come down the opposite bank for a drink, she crouched down slowly before the animal could see her. Then moments later, the same animal that had been calmly drinking water, suddenly jumped into the puddle and charged straight for her across the river bed.

The friend covered her head with her arms and balled up. Behind her, one of her camp mates ran from the forest yelling and brandishing a tree branch, but the bear showed no sign of slowing down. Another quick-thinking companion fired his gun at the ground in front of the bear.

The noise and spray of sand hitting its face brought the creature to an abrupt halt. A moment later, it turned around and loped back into the forest. None of us can explain why the bear attacked. After hearing this story, I'm much less certain that the stick I carry would deter an intent bear.

Yet, despite the occasional unpredictable danger posed by wild animals, it is far riskier driving in the city. Few people follow traffic rules, and impatience, road rage and recklessness rule.

Take Me Home

Rom's mother always said that a toad or two under the kitchen sink was all one needed to keep the house clean of cockroaches. Much like everything else on our crazy farm, toads just colonized our house *en masse*. At night I had to watch every step, like walking on a forest path. No matter how careful I was, the magnificently-sized, sticky toad turds jumped out, and stuck themselves to the soles of my feet. Dropping whatever I was doing, I was forced to hobble off to wash the offending black 'toad-gum' immediately. After a while, I threw the toads out of the house, but fearlessly they returned to face my wrath.

I collected the toads in a plastic container, took them to the edge of the front yard, about 250 metres away, and released them. They had the temerity to return. I marked them with a marking pen (identification), spun the container round and round (disorientation, I thought), took them on a long detour around the farm (confusing, I imagined) before letting them go 500 metres away. 'There!' I proclaimed in smug confidence. They were back in 25 hours.

By now, the blighters knew what was in store when the she-ogre came for them. They squeaked in distress, pissed copiously in fright, and tried to evade capture. I almost relented, but now curiosity drove me on. 750 metres. Back in 30 hours. That's a fairly long distance for small creatures to navigate. I spun the bottle, took them down the long dirt path, across the road, into the jungle and let them go by a puddle. One kilometre away. Success? While I succeeded in chasing them out of the house, days later I found a couple with telltale markings in the outdoor planters. Now I can't tell if all of them made it back or only some did. What do other creatures do when taken far from home? Here are some interesting facts I unearthed.

In Namibia, 11 marked leopards were moved 800 very long kilometres away. Six returned home over a period of 5 to 25 months. Let me put it this way – if these cats had been taken from Chennai and released north of Goa, they were able to walk right back. In the US, most of the 34 black bears that were moved about 200 kms from their home territories returned successfully. In India, an elephant translocated from the Terai to Buxa Tiger Reserve, a distance of about 250 kms, returned in less than two months. Salt water crocodiles in Australia were shown to home back after being moved 400 kms. Put me anywhere in Bangalore, and I'm lost immediately.

However, the distance record for homing is held by seabirds such as albatrosses and shearwaters. An albatross taken from an island in the Central Pacific, and released about 6,500 kms away in the Philippines returned in a month; two others returned from Washington State, US, 5,000 kms away.

It is not just the larger animals that possess this amazing skill. In the UK, bumblebees found their way home after being randomly dropped off 13 kms away from their hives. So what's a kilometre to a toad, eh?

The fact that these animals, birds, and insects return home is well-documented. But how do they find their way through unfamiliar terrain over long distances?

Since these animals are frequently moved in covered vehicles (or a closed plastic container) on the outward journey, it is unlikely they remember the route. In many cases, the animals' return journey did not follow the road they were taken out on at all, but instead took a more direct path homewards. How do they do it?

You need two things to find your way to a place – a map and a compass. The first shows your current location in relation to your destination, and the second tells you the direction you are moving. Biologists believe that animals have these instruments hard-wired in their brains and sensory organs.

Navigation in homing pigeons was studied for over half a century. Since the sense of sight is useful only if you are in a familiar place, experimenters wondered if pigeons used the sun to navigate. Shifting the birds' body clock by artificially lighting their lofts at night and darkening them during the day neutralizes this solar navigation system. When released on sunny days, the unfortunate birds were disoriented, and couldn't find their way home. But on overcast days, they had no problems at all, because in the absence of the sun, they may have relied on another navigation system.

Perhaps they were using the earth's magnetic field. Like many birds and animals, pigeons have magnetite (or iron oxide) particles in the upper part of their beaks. We have a single crystal between our eyes and behind the nose, and minute crystals in the brain. These particles may help the animals sense the earth's magnetic field, like a compass. To deactivate this sense, experimenters attached magnets to the birds' heads, and anesthetized their upper beaks. Such magnet-neutralized birds got lost on overcast days because they couldn't navigate using the magnetic field or the sun. On sunny days, they found their way to the loft. If deprived of one sense, the pigeons appear to be compensating with another.

An American geologist, Jon Hagstrum, came up with yet another theory to explain how birds are able to tell where they are. The earth's crust is thought to emit a constant, low frequency infrasound. Like the magnetic field, every part of the planet has its own sonic signature. Hagstrum says some birds may be able to hear these infrasounds and recognize where they are. Some others suggest smell may play a part, while others disagree. So the jury is still out. Whether animals use sight, smell, sun, stars, the earth's magnetic field, infrasound or a combination of these remains a magical mystery.

I should mention that homing pigeons are selectively bred for their remarkable ability to return home from hundreds of kilometres away. In other words, it is a genetic trait; some have it and others don't. Likewise, not all animals that are displaced find their way home; some get lost and wander aimlessly.

Over the years, Rom and I have argued over who has the better sense of direction, just like so many others. But one exceptional field researcher, J. Vijaya, had a remarkable sense of direction. Shekar Dattatri, the wildlife filmmaker, says Vijaya would wander through an unfamiliar forest without notching a tree or snapping a branch, and yet unerringly find her way back. We don't know how she did it, and it's now too late to ask because she died in 1987.

Back home, this homing instinct backfired when our war on the Croc Bank ants began in earnest. I remembered Ma-in-law's dictum as well as our previous experience at the Croc Bank. Grudgingly, I caught two toads from the garden, and left them under the sink. They wouldn't have any of it; they ran back into the garden at the first opportunity. Feeling like the shamefaced princess who had to kiss the toad, I gave them a nice, cozy little cardboard box. They didn't want that either. So I swore that the next toad which came into the house would get red carpet treatment, stinky scats notwithstanding. I'll even kiss the creature if need be, as long as it takes care of the ants from hell.

The Endangered Scrub Jungle

What did the original forests around Chengalpattu, south of Chennai, look like before they were cut down to make way for agriculture centuries ago?

For much of my life, the nearest wilderness areas – Guindy National Park in Chennai and the campus of the Madras Christian College – were called 'scrub forest'. It didn't inspire respect like 'rainforest' or 'deciduous forest'; it seemed more like a poor country cousin. I assumed that the forest around our farm was also 'scrub'.

Then botanists from Auroville, the international township not far from us, drew up an inventory of the trees and plants found in the forest adjacent to our farm. Surprisingly, the list included satinwood, ebony, and bullet wood. These were huge timber trees that ought to have been 15 to 20 metres high but were no more than stunted bushes, the result of continuous hacking for fodder and firewood. What were these giants doing here? I wondered. The botanists said this was a 'tropical dry evergreen forest'. I had never heard of it before. The experts added that the dry evergreen forests were even more endangered than rainforests; only an estimated four to five per cent of the original forest remains. How very typical; we fretted about distant rainforests, when the forest under our noses was in worse shape.

The tropical dry evergreen forest formed a strip about 30 to 60 km wide along the Southeastern coast of India. Large parts of this area were settled and cleared for agriculture about two millennia ago. Only fragments of forest remain protected as reserve forest and sacred groves.

Being categorized as reserve forest, the wild area adjoining our farm received the bare minimum protection. Armed with long lists of trees, reptiles, mammals, and birds and with all the zealousness of a conservationist, Rom lobbied the forest department to provide greater protection to a 40 km swathe of forests from Vandalur, on the periphery of Chennai, to the Palar River. The forest was nearly contiguous except for a few gaps. Greater protection meant declaring a sanctuary, the officials demurred; there were too many villages and people in the way, they said.

However, Rom's lobbying did not fail completely. The forest department included our village under the Joint Forestry Management Programme. The scheme was intended to wean people off the forest by providing gas cylinders and milch cows, and growing fodder trees on village commons. Two years later, the change was dramatic.

Trees began to emerge head and shoulders above shrubs. The bald silhouette of the hill against the setting sun began to appear woollier. Paths through the forest became overgrown and impassable.

When the funds ran dry, some people went back to exploiting the forest, but not as much as they did prior to the programme. There was just not enough manpower left in villages to herd goats or cut firewood. People were migrating to the city in search of better opportunities.

We joined our fellow tree planters in rubbing our hands with glee; urban migration was going to solve all the problems we faced in regenerating the countryside. The fact that city people use far more resources that had to be brought from further and further away was an inconvenient fact that did not tarnish the impending victory.

I can only imagine what the original forest of Chengalpattu may have been like. There are no records and no pockets of pristine vegetation. Guindy National Park became the reference point and aspirational goal.

Soon after the civil war ended in Sri Lanka, we visited Wilpattu National Park, which had been closed to visitors until then. Spread over 1,300 sq kms, the trees were familiar in name but unfamiliar in numbers and girth. Sloth bear scats at regular intervals on the main dirt road, cannon ball-sized elephant dung, a leopard, mugger crocodiles, and an array of creatures big and small, were the highlights of the memorable day.

My vision of the Chengalpattu forests' future grandeur climbed loftier heights. Instead of Guindy National Park, I now aspired for Wilpattu's stature. Our home forest had a leopard. Elephants could possibly make the approximately 150 km hike from Tirupati or Hosur. Sloth bears could feel at home in the rocky caves on the hills.

As I assessed the possibilities of future colonization of the Chengalpattu forests by these animals, Rom interrupted my wistful dreaming, 'The city is definitely creeping our

way, and we are enjoying the best years of the place.'

Thud! It was a nice dream while it lasted.

Bird Impersonators

Very early one morning in the Andamans, we were woken up by the persistent yowling of two tomcats fighting. Bleary-eyed, I walked out onto the balcony, and looked down the forested slope. A few moments later, to my amazement, I realized that it was a greater racket-tailed drongo mimicking both sides of the catty argument. Shaking my head in disbelief, I listened to the bird's full repertoire. From fighting tomcats, the bird moved on to the piercing call of a white-bellied sea eagle before going onto the sweet chirps of a tailor bird interspersed with a discordant truck horn. What was the point of this extraordinary mimicry?

Greater racket-tailed drongos hunt in feeding parties made of several species of birds. Sri Lankan ornithologists theorized that drongos may mimic different species to invite them to form such a group. But we don't know for sure if this is coincidence or deliberate use of mimicry. Besides, mimicking tomcats was an unlikely invitation to a party.

While other birds are engrossed in foraging, drongos may act as sentinels, watching for predators. Should danger lurk, they sometimes mimic the alarm calls of various birds, presumably to incite a mob attack. But drongos appear to mix up alarm and non-alarm calls.

A while ago, we witnessed a black drongo making loud shikra calls, even as the latter was feeding on a golden oriole chick within earshot. The neat trick certainly didn't drive the shikra away. Was it intentionally trying to incite a mob attack? It is also possible that if a drongo picks up a sound when it is stressed, it will tend to mimic that sound when it is under duress again.

Famously, some species like parrots and hill mynas have learnt to talk. This aptitude may be reinforced as their human trainers reward them when they say the right thing. But parrots can imitate a vacuum cleaner, a ringing telephone, and even a barking dog without the benefit of such treats. Einstein, a famous African grey parrot at the Knoxville zoo, imitates wolves, chimpanzees, roosters, tigers, and a range of other animal neighbours. Of what use could such remarkable mimicry be in the forest where wild parrots live?

Laura Kelley at Deakin University in Australia says that parrots in the wild live in flocks, and mimic each other to strengthen their social bonding. In captivity, they imitate the next best thing to a flock, their human or animal companions.

The most spectacular bird mimic, the lyrebird, is a hit on YouTube. It can imitate a car reversing, camera shutter, chain saw, the sound of falling trees, rifle shots, musical instruments, fire alarms, crying babies, trains, humans, just about anything it hears. Since male birds go to great lengths mimicking human sounds during the breeding season, ornithologists suggest that females may be selecting males with the most complex song. But European biologists found no evidence that male songbirds with better imitating skills have their way with the ladies. Another, somewhat nihilistic, theory suggests that mimicry may just be a learning error which serves no ultimate purpose.

Scientists reported that the drongos of the Kalahari make fake alarm calls to steal someone else's lunch. When the birds noticed a meerkat or babbler with a tidbit of food, they cried wolf. When the scared animal or bird ran for cover, dropping its prey in haste, the drongos were quick to snatch it. So far this deception is the only proven function for vocal mimicry.

Could the miaowing racket-tailed drongo in the Andamans have been trying to wrest a tidbit? Or did it feel threatened by a cat on the prowl perhaps? I can't imagine the acrobatic bird would have been threatened by a truck or the tiny tailor bird.

Kelley cautions that the art of mimicry is widespread around the world, and there may be no single explanation.

In the meantime, I marvel at birds' abilities to add dishwashers and ambulances to their repertoire, using the environment as a living, vibrant musical alphabet.

Snake-bite 'Heroes'

Rom's arm was swollen and throbbed with pain. Instead of commiserating with him, his friends cursed and made fun of him. He was so embarrassed, he felt like crawling under a log and disappearing.

It was the mid-1960s. Rom and his friends went looking for snakes in the Everglades, Florida. On one occasion, Rom spied a venomous water moccasin on a log in the water. As he pinned its head, the floating log sank a little. If he let go of the snake to make another attempt, it would dive into the water. So the stupid boy grabbed it anyway . . . *bam*!

After bagging the snake, Rom confessed to Schubert Lee, his snake-hunting partner, 'Hey man, a moccasin bit me.'

Without a pause in his stride, or concern in his voice, Schubert drawled in his Southern accent, 'Yup, they do that sometimes.'

Soon the arm became very swollen, and the two had to call it quits. Schubert quietly cursed Rom for ruining a good snakey day.

With great disdain, Rom's boss, Bill Haast of the Miami Serpentarium, gave him a day off. Other friends commented, 'An obvious learner,' or, 'Trying to impress the girls, you dumb [*bleep*]?' It's the kind of response an electrician who gets an electric shock would receive from his colleagues. Or anyone who clearly didn't know his job very well. Rom was so harassed by the aggressive teasing that the lesson stayed with him for life.

Another time, one of Rom's friends was changing the water dish in a western diamondback rattlesnake's terrarium, when it bit his hand.

The now-wise Rom asked, 'But why didn't you put the snake into another box first?'

Attila replied, 'It was looking the other way, so I figured I could quietly do my job.'

At this, everyone burst out laughing even though their friend was rocking back and forth nursing a very painful arm. Someone did drive him to the hospital eventually.

If a snake-catcher gets bitten by a venomous snake, it is his own fault. He was careless, most probably trying to show off, and wasn't paying attention. That was the motto of Rom and his snake-hunting buddies in the US during the '60s, and it still holds true. In keeping with that philosophy, anyone who gets bit in our circle of colleagues is teased mercilessly. Non-snake-hunting civilians bitten accidentally are exempt, of course. There is no doubt that this tradition of peer admonition has kept these men, most of them, alive to this day.

In India, however, numerous snake-catchers, invariably young men, brag about their various snakebite 'exploits'.

One bright spark bagged a cobra in a flimsy, translucent bag. When he moved in closer to knot it, the snake nailed him on the hand through the cloth. He was in hospital for a few days, and in the Indian tradition, the entire neighbourhood crowded around his bedside to express its concern. Basking in all this attention, our man never once paused to think why the incident had occurred.

When he bragged about it numerous times, Rom asked him, 'Whose fault was it?'

The young man didn't seem sure. 'But it was certainly not my fault,' he declared.

Rom countered, 'If you had used a proper bag to begin with, you wouldn't have been bit, right? So tell me now, whose fault was it?'

Silence.

When I was editing the Croc Bank newsletter, a large number of articles submitted for publication were on snakebite experiences. One was even titled *The Badge of Courage*, which I was sorely tempted to change to *The Badge of Stupidity*. These survivors don't realize that their survival depends on two things – how much venom the snake injects and the skill of doctors. By getting bit, these snake molesters, as we now call them, haven't really done anything to deserve boasting rights, except being plain, outright inept. That's like a carpenter who misses the head of a nail and smashes his thumb, bragging about what a cool dude he is.

Should any of your snake-catching buddies suffer a bite and survive, please don't throng his bedside and go 'ooh' and 'aah'. Instead, if you really care about him, tease him mercilessly. It will go a long way in prolonging his lifespan.

The Case of the
Mythical Malabar Civet

The two large civets were crunching up chicken bones, leftovers of the forest guards' dinner that had been thrown into the elephant trench surrounding the building. The animals seemed much bigger than the common small Indian civets. Every now and then they stood on their hind legs to get a better perspective of us. We had the same thought – Malabar civet. We made no move to get a camera for fear they would run away. Instead, that night in the High Wavy Mountains, we tried to memorize the civet's features in the dark.

Almost six decades earlier, Angus Hutton, a tea planter in the adjoining tea estate, had recorded that the Malabar civet was 'very common'. By 1939, it was feared the Malabar civet was close to extinction. We were excited to have seen such a highly endangered creature.

However, Ajith Kumar of the Centre for Wildlife Studies doubted we had seen the species. It's likely we saw the commoner small Indian civet, he said. There was tremendous variation in features, pattern, and size of the species depending on the habitat, altitude, and latitude.

One biologist asked if the civets we had seen had a mane. We hadn't noticed. Three stripes along the throat? We thought we saw something like that. Another asked if we noticed whether the bands completely encircled the tail. Don't know, it was too dark. Did they have black tail tips? Huh? Unfortunately, we hadn't known to look for these features.

Years later, R. Nandini and Divya Mudappa, two experts on small mammals, published an account of their investigations on the Malabar civet. They examined six skins and three skulls held in various museums in the UK and India, and pored over everything ever written by wildlife experts from the 1800s onwards.

Thomas Jerdon, an eminent zoologist of the 19th century, said he thought the Malabar civet was found in the lowland coastal forests of the Western Ghats from Honavar, Northern Karnataka, to Trivandrum, Kerala. Since then subsequent mammalogists have repeated this as fact. A few animals were seen far inland in Biligiri Rangaswamy Temple Wildlife Sanctuary, Tirunelveli, and in the High Wavy Mountains. But most of the records were around Kozhikode, Kerala. No other civet cat in Asia is so narrowly restricted in range.

Nandini and Divya agreed there was a possibility the Malabar civet may have become extremely rare from being hunted for its famous musk. But the extensive loss of coastal forests was also blamed. Could the animals really be so finicky that they couldn't tolerate the conversion of their forests to plantations? No other species of civet is so fussy about the changing vegetation.

What does a Malabar civet look like? There is no clarity because the origin of museum specimens is obscure, and mammalogists contradict each other. To confuse matters further, the large-spotted civet of Southeast Asia and the Malabar civet look almost identical.

Over millennia, civets were traded between Ethiopia, Southeast Asia and India for civetone, a secretion of the anal musk glands used in traditional medicine, perfumery, and as a religious offering. Even today, small Indian civets are maintained on farms in Tirupati, Andhra Pradesh, for the extraction of musk. Kozhikode, the centre of most recent Malabar civet records, was a well-known trading port from ancient times.

Nandini and Divya wondered if there was a possibility large-spotted civets brought from Southeast Asia escaped from captivity leading to occasional observation in the wild. This is not so far-fetched, as captive small Indian civets have escaped and established themselves in countries such as Madagascar, Philippines, and other islands of Southeast Asia.

It is distinctly possible the Malabar civet as a species does not exist. Only genetic analysis, currently underway, can tell us for sure.

Excited by our report of seeing Malabar civets in the High Wavy Mountains, Kerala Forest Department officials visited the spot, and confirmed the animals we had seen were indeed small Indian civets. Our initial exuberance on seeing a long-lost species turned to disappointment on hearing this news.

Immaculate Reptilian Conceptions

Every now and then, reptiles reveal a miraculous facility that takes my breath away. One such talent that some species possess is to reproduce without a male partner, which scientists call 'parthenogenesis' (Greek for 'virgin birth'). Females of the little house geckos found in our homes can give birth without males. Others such as the butterfly lizard in Vietnam and the New Mexico whiptail lizard in the US have gone one step further and completely eliminated males from their populations. No males have ever been found.

All lizards that procreate by parthenogenesis alone are hybrids of other sexually reproducing species. Not only has the definition of what makes a species become blurred, but here is a case of a new one being created without taking thousands of evolutionary years.

The most widespread snake in the world is the miniscule Brahminy worm snake. It is the only all-female snake species, and researchers haven't yet determined if it is a hybrid.

We thought fatherless births occur in just small creatures. Imagine our surprise when we heard of a two-and-a-half-foot captive timber rattlesnake in Colorado called Marsha Joan producing a son, Napoleon, in 1995. She had never met a male in her 14-year lifetime. The following decade saw immaculate conception occur in a Burmese python called Maria in The Netherlands, and Aruba Island rattlesnakes in the US.

Appropriately, close to Christmas 2006, seven baby Komodo dragons were born to Flora at the Chester Zoo, UK. The seven-year-old mother dragon had never met a male. Another Komodo, Sungai, at the London Zoo had been producing babies two years after her last contact with a male Komodo. On hearing of Flora's miraculous progeny, genetic tests of Sungai's offspring revealed that Sungai was also producing copies of herself without the aid of sex. Babies of such single parents are usually male because of their unique sex chromosomes.

In 2010, scientists announced that Caramel, a beautiful caramel-coloured Colombian boa constrictor at The Boa Store, a pet shop in Tennessee, US, had produced 22 babies parthenogenetically. Amazingly, she shared her enclosure with four males. Owner, Sharon Moore says they suspected something was up when all the babies had the same extraordinary colouration, which is caused by a recessive gene. Under normal, sexual circumstances, only a few in a clutch would inherit a rare trait. Paternity tests clinched the case. However, Caramel was no virgin; she had sexually reproduced before.

Two Ganges softshell turtles at the Croc Bank have been laying fertile eggs for the last 15 years without a male. Female turtles are known to store sperm in special receptacles for a few years. But now, after learning about Caramel, Flora, Maria and Sungai, it appears that virgin birth may not be such a rare phenomenon in the reptile world. Whether it is sperm storage or parthenogenesis, these turtles have created history. This is the longest period of sperm storage known for any vertebrate in the world. Alternately, if tests prove it, they may be the first turtles capable of immaculate conception.

The boa constrictor Caramel's case was extraordinary on another count as well – her babies were all female. Until now, it was thought that parthenogenetic daughters in normally sexual species could happen only in a lab using complicated techniques. It's ironic that the serpent, an animal that supposedly revealed carnal knowledge to humans in the Garden of Eden, should itself be capable of asexual reproduction.

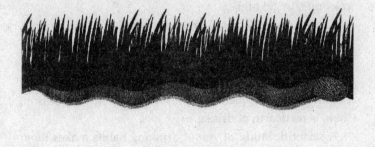

Riding High

One thing that every human civilization around the world has in common is an intoxicant. Some substances are considered sacred, but most frequently, we simply drink to celebrate, to get high.

Getting stoned is not a human prerogative. Many animals go to great lengths to get a fix. In Tamil Nadu, bonnet macaques are occasional raiders of illegal stills secreted in forests. While in the Caribbean, vervet Monkeys have become regular tipplers. With a year-round holiday season, there is no dearth of drinks.

A scientific study of vervet drinking habits makes them seem surprisingly human. A few binge drinkers chug it down fast, hard, and often, while steady drinkers like their booze neat and regularly. Most are social drinkers who prefer cocktails, while some remain teetotallers. The resemblances don't stop there. Some get heavy and aggressive when drunk, a few get horny, while others turn morose. Most, however, just get happily sozzled, perhaps seeing pink elephants.

Regular elephants of the dark kind are known to go berserk after a drink too many. In December 2010, a herd of

70 Asian elephants gate-crashed a village party, and became so drunk on hooch that they went on a four-day rampage on the West Bengal-Orissa border. A couple of years earlier, another herd that went on a binge knocked down electric posts, frying itself in the process.

Cats in the temperate West get high on catnip. They roll on the stems of this mint plant over and over again, drooling and moaning. When I gave some to my father's cat, which had never seen the herb before, he went nuts. But a few minutes later, he became completely sober and walked off with dignity. During a visit to an American zoo, we witnessed a cougar acting silly with a catnip stuffed sock; apparently many cats are susceptible to the herb.

In the Rocky Mountains, big-horned sheep are known to climb up precarious cliffs to scrape a particular kind of lichen that grows on rocks to get a buzz, while in Yemen, goats are addicted to *khat* leaves, just like their herders.

Fly agaric mushrooms are the pretty, red-capped, candy-like toadstools that innocently illustrate many children's books. Despite their alarming don't-eat-me colours, reindeer do eat them and get as high as kites. Since most of the toxins are filtered by the animals' kidneys, drinking their urine is apparently safer than eating the mushrooms. And that is what high-seeking herders in Northern Europe and Asia do.

One of the numerous stories of Santa Claus' origins leads to Siberia. During a mid-winter festival, a shaman enters the yurt through the central smoke-hole, carrying a bag of dried fly agaric mushrooms. Santa wears the colours of the toadstool and rides reindeer which appear to be flying. When people are zonked on these 'shrooms', their faces, especially cheeks and nose, turn ruddy. No prizes for guessing what Santa and Rudolph are high on while riding through the sky!

Through the centuries, society has sought to outlaw these substances as dangerous and evil. Yet, indulging in them may well be as firmly entrenched in our genes as in our customs. Even children seek a high by whirling round and round until they are unsteady on their feet. Dervishes use a similar technique to gain an out-of-mind spiritual experience. This is where Edward de Bono, who developed the concept of 'lateral thinking', takes off. He suggests that intoxicants can help you think creatively by taking you out of your set pattern of thinking. If that were true, surely the world will see a spate of new ideas, inventions, and endeavours as an offshoot of the mind-altering experiences of New Year's Eve.

The Beast Within

When the sun moves from *Dhanus* (Sagittarius) to *Makara* (Capricorn), marking the end of the winter solstice, we celebrate *Makara Sankranti*. Makara means sea monster in Sanskrit and is the origin of the word 'mugger', both in Hindi and English. In Hindu iconography, makara is also represented as the *vahana* (vehicle) of Ma Ganga, the river goddess.

The master sculptor, V. Ganapati Sthapati, describes makara as a mythical animal with the body of a fish, trunk of an elephant, feet of a lion, eyes of a monkey, ears of a pig, and the tail of a peacock. Although it seems improbable, these disparate elements come together to form one of the commonest leitmotifs in Indian temple iconography. A line of makara may run along the length of a temple wall, or form the hand rail of a staircase. But most prominently, this beast acts as structural bookend of a *thoranam* or archway behind a deity. The arch issues forth from the jaws of one makara, rises to a pinnacle called the *kirtimukha* (the 'Face of Glory'), and descends into the yawning gape of another makara.

The fabulous beast isn't just an adornment; it apparently

symbolizes chaos out of which order and creation arise. The height of order is depicted by the fearsome kirtimukha, and then creation descends once more into chaos. The deity sitting in front of the archway presides over the eternal cycle of creation and destruction.

Folk artists of old didn't buy into this metaphysical symbolism; instead they depicted the makara as a real animal. They found gharial in the thousands basking along the banks of the Ganges and other North Indian rivers and appropriated it as Ma Ganga's vehicle. The mythical creature's elephant trunk does resemble a stylized gharial snout.

Kirtimukha, at the top of the arch, has a lion's snarling face with fearsome bulging eyes, a tongue hanging out, bared teeth, and occasionally a pair of horns. In the legend, when a vainglorious king had the temerity to lay claim on Siva's beautiful wife, a terrible demon issued fully formed from the wrathful god's third eye. The petrified messenger of the king fell at Siva's feet begging for mercy and the god forgave him. But the ogre had been born with a raging hunger that had to be appeased. On the god's orders, it ate its own body until only the head remained (similar in theme to the Ouroboros, the snake swallowing its tail). Impressed by this obedient self-cannibalism, Siva proclaimed that henceforth the demon-head would be known as kirtimukha and worshipped in all his temples.

Joseph Campbell, the late eminent mythologist, opined that the story of kirtimukha reveals the fundamental Truth – life lives off death. Everyday we see folksy versions painted on construction sites, on ash gourds, on the backs of trucks, and as masks for scarecrows to ward off the 'evil eye'.

Today, the last 200 breeding gharial try to bask and nest on river banks gouged by rampant sand mining and farming. The Yamuna and Ganga may be holy rivers, but they are also among the most polluted in the world. More than 100 gharial died in the winter of 2007-08 from toxin-caused kidney failure in the Chambal, a Yamuna tributary, caused by a suspected pollutant.

At least kirtimukha was divinely directed to self-destruction. What compels us humans to gobble and destroy our way through earth's resources until there is no tomorrow? Are we hell-bent on sending this unique life-sustaining planet to Saturn, the haunted house of Hindu astrology? In the story, kirtimukha may be a parable of life. In reality, wouldn't you say that it holds a mirror to the grotesque face of our rapaciousness?

In December 2010, in a bid to give the gharial a fighting chance of survival, Jairam Ramesh, the then Minister of Environment and Forests, pledged his ministry's support for this crocodilian's conservation. Perhaps we can truly now say, Happy Makara Sankranti!

Wildlife Idols

Jim Corbett's books left a lasting impression on many people who love wildlife. Occasionally, I hear Kenneth Anderson mentioned as an influence as well. But neither of these two writers inspired my fixation on wildlife. It was Enid Blyton. Her non-fiction books on the English countryside were my unlikely source of inspiration.

I remember as a 10-year-old setting out a large plate of water for a birdbath on the terrace of our home in the city of Madras and being distinctly disappointed when ordinary old house crows arrived. What did I expect? Pipits and robins? Yes!

Then I set up a feeding station hoping for a range of exotic seed-eating birds. But palm squirrels, those pesky 'tree rats', demolished it all. The impoverished landscape of the city didn't offer much scope for wildlife exploration, especially British birds!

From Blyton I learnt the difference between hares and rabbits, toads and frogs, about bees and seeds, and flowers and weeds. I was enthralled. Her instructions on how to approach wildlife – slowly, without a noise, barely even breathing – still stand me in good stead.

In the absence of wild animals, I honed these skills on the neighbours' cats. If I saw one in the backyard, I would stalk it, crouching low as I approached, never making eye contact, and would woo the feral creature while it grew more and more suspicious.

After all these years, it embarrasses me that I spent so much time cultivating these domesticated predators. Now, living on our farm surrounded by 'real' birds and animals, I truly feel sorry for city kids who do not have that contact with nature. Perhaps I'm really only feeling sad for my own childhood self.

In my teens I became besotted with Gerald Durrell. I read and re-read his books, savoured his wit and concern for animals large and small, and my world-view was solidly cemented.

I was in my twenties when I finally ventured into Jim Corbett and Kenneth Anderson territory. Their fixation on the hunting of large charismatic mammals left me completely indifferent, maybe even repulsed. Perhaps reacting subconsciously to the projection of their macho personae, I turned my back on large cats, becoming more enamoured by snakes, frogs, millipedes, laughing thrushes, and dung beetles. You could argue that they were at least talking about Indian wildlife. But to a Madras-grown girl, the Deccan and Kumaon were as foreign as England.

Years later, Rom and I set up Draco Films to make documentaries about some of these little-known creatures, mainly reptiles. In an ironic twist, within a couple of years, snakes became the next sexy, macho animal on television!

The new rage produced a glut of films that idolized men jumping on venomous snakes around the world. From decades of investment in 'blue chip' animal behaviour, the focus of television channels moved to celebrity wildlife 'wranglers'. Where we had spent 10 to 12 months following and filming animals for one film during the 90s, entire films were now made in little more than 10 weeks.

True, the audience was able to connect with animals more viscerally when there was a personality on screen. We proposed a compromise – some human interest mixed with animal behaviour. After a couple of such films, the executives gave the thumbs down. They wanted more presenter time on screen and little of animals behaving naturally. 'Churn 'em out' was the new motto at most of the big animal channels.

When my growing aversion to this new genre of wildlife documentaries reached a peak, I quit film-making. My preference for Enid Blyton and Gerald Durrell over Jim Corbett clearly offered parallels to the way I saw the new, exaggerated style of presenting wildlife. In an effort to figure out what I could do next, I reached back to the roots of my own interest in animals, and that was how I began writing about my experiences with wildlife.

Spare That Rod

Ever since *The Wall Street Journal* ran an excerpt of Amy Chua's memoirs in early January 2011 describing her authoritarian way of bringing up her children, websites and blogs have gone berserk with opinions on the 'traditional Chinese' style parenting. Alas, we Indians are no less draconian.

My childhood wasn't easy, neither for me nor my parents. Exam results and teacher evaluations were the unwavering focus throughout my growing up years. The days when my report card had to be signed by a parent and returned to the teacher were a special ordeal. Forget good marks, I did everything else – forged Mother's signature (easier than studying), lied through my teeth, and accused the teacher of vendetta – just to avoid being punished. The whole system was built on fear and avoidance, rather than encouragement and learning.

In later years, I raised several dogs in the tradition that I had been brought up in. I house-trained them by rubbing their noses in their piss, scolding them when they shat, stepped on their toes if they jumped on me, whacked them with rolled up newspapers, and, if they were really naughty, locked them in the kennel. Eventually they learnt right and wrong, as I did decades ago.

Some years ago, I woke up late one morning to find Karadi, our German shepherd, sitting in the kennel. Odd! Even the racket of the other mutts greeting Rom and me did not bring him out. Both of us called him affectionately, only to be ignored. Something was up.

Later that morning, my parents, who live next door, said Karadi had jumped the fence and paid them a visit. He knew he had done wrong and had punished himself! This carried on for a few days. The dog knew the price for being naughty and was willing to pay it. Now what could I do? He obviously figured that the fun of being mischievous far outweighed the punishment.

Clearly the training wasn't working. So I did some research and discovered that my methods were archaic. Almost overnight I switched strategy to positive reinforcement – reward good behaviour and ignore the bad. If a not-yet-house-trained puppy does his job in the garden, he gets cuddled and praised. But if he has an accident inside the house, I just clean up. No anger, no shouting, no whacking. To my astonishment, the dogs learnt very quickly.

There are two different processes here – rules and enforcement. The first remains as strict as they always were; the only thing that changed was the training. Until they learn the basic rules in all its forms, I am strict – jumping on us is not allowed, neither is jumping on the postman or guests. When I reinforce these rules with rewards (using treats, affection or play), I am making it difficult for them to disobey. Even our 'un-trainable' Chippiparai now bows on command.

But there is one situation where I negatively-condition the dogs. Venomous snakes are a danger to dogs on farms. We let a bitey, non-venomous watersnake caught from our pond bite the noses of our puppies. It is momentarily painful, but they learn a valuable life-saving lesson – stay far away from snakes. It's not a situation when I want them to feel happy or playful; I want them to panic and recoil. In all other situations, I reward good behaviour.

I'll let you in on a little insight – it works even on grown men! As in most Western potty households, Rom and I had our share of endless toilet-seat arguments. It was a no-win situation, until one day, after I learnt positive reinforcement, I found the seat down and a light bulb went on in my head. I gave Rom a loving squeeze and lo, thenceforth the seat was flipped down oftener than it was up. Besides, it is so much more fun to cuddle than argue.

The Cyclone of 85

Winter is cyclone season on the Madras coast. I'm reminded of the last bad one to hit Chennai. Was it 1985? All I recall is being stuck at home, bored and waterlogged, after exhausting all options of electricity-less entertainment.

For Rom, however, at the Croc Bank, it was a harrowing 48-hour drama. At dusk on the first day of the cyclone, he remembers trying to stand upright on the beach when the wind gauge was clocking 120 kmph and rising. The skies looked ominous and more serious weather was on its way.

Then for 24 hours rain belted down. The water level in the croc enclosures began rising steadily until there was no high ground left. The crocs were swimming round and round along the edge. Some of the enclosure walls were only of single brick thickness, not strong enough to withstand the pressure of the water. Before they caved in, Rom and his staff punched holes in the walls to relieve the strain. There was no predicting what else was in store, so 20 trusty villagers were hired to keep a watch on the crocs. Each was armed with an aptly named hurricane lamp and a stout stick. It was a long tiring night of deafening wind, pouring rain and menacing surf.

By noon the next day, the wind had died down, but the Croc Bank was strewn with piles of debris. On the beach, enormous trunks of trees from far-off shores lay washed up like beached walruses. The Kovalam Bridge was submerged under a torrent of rushing water and the road to Kelambakkam had disappeared. Apart from a thin strip of coastal road, a sheet of water covered everything. The Croc Bank was marooned for three days. Had high tide coincided with the cyclone hitting the coast, Madras city would have been devastated.

To add to the chaos, a tom-tom messenger went from village to village announcing that a thousand crocodiles had escaped from the Croc Bank, and cautioning people not to go near water. How exactly does one do that when the whole place is flooded?

Although there was no evidence that so many crocs had disappeared from the Croc Bank, the worry of escapees was never far from Rom's mind. But there was too much to do at the Croc Bank and there was a shortage of manpower.

The crocs seemed bewildered by the sound and light show that had changed the profile of their enclosures. But the worst was over and now it was just a matter of cleaning up. After a long day of back-breaking work, a deeply-asleep Rom was awakened by the incessant barking of Balu, the watch dog.

A large male gharial had escaped and was crawling through the casuarina grove to the sea. Rom picked up a fallen branch and fenced with the 13-foot crocodile to keep it at bay. Balu was barking and excitedly prancing around, staying just out of reach of the gharial's tooth-lined snout. Rom's shouts for help were drowned by the roar of the surf.

Man and dog could only slow the reptile's progress to the sea.

As Rom considered his diminishing options, the night security staff finally showed up. With additional manpower and gear, the gharial was hauled off to the safety of its enclosure. It transpired that the receding water had left a pile of sand at one corner which the clean-up crew had failed to notice. So the intrepid gharial had merely climbed up the mound, jumped over the wall and followed the sound of waves to the sea.

Once the croc enclosures had been cleaned up, the staff went out into the surrounding villages to eye-shine for crocs (since crocs' eyes reflect torchlight at night, this is the standard method of finding them), and scan the land for tracks. There wasn't even one croc on the loose, never mind a thousand. Rom didn't find the source of this misinformation and eventually everything went back to normal.

Had the gharial made good its escape, it would have been a public relations disaster.

Devil Nettle

When I set foot in a new forest, I always request, 'Show me the nettles first.' In my experience, the one with the worst reputation is called devil nettle, fever nettle or elephant nettle, and its scientific name is *Dendrocnide sinuata* (meaning 'tree nettle' with 'wavy leaf margin' in Greek). It is found in the forests of the Western Ghats, the Northeast and onwards into Southeast Asia.

I was first introduced to this plant in Manjolai near the Kalakkad-Mundanthurai Tiger Reserve (Tamil Nadu) where they call it '*Anaimeratti*' (Tamil for 'that which threatens elephants'). The leaves of most nettles have a distinctive shape and hairy texture, but not the devil nettle. It looks like any other innocuous plant with dark green oval leaves. The minute irritating hairs covering the leaves are visible only when you are about two inches from it. Wherever there is a forest opening with lots of sunlight, one is likely to see this plant which can grow to the size of a small tree. I tried hard to memorize its non-distinctive features, but even today I cannot identify it with certainty. That's probably because I've never been stung by it.

When Rom first visited Agumbe in the early 1970s, he

had some peculiar ideas. He felt that all the trappings of the human world interfered with his ability to find king cobras. So he discarded his watch and shoes, and stripped down to a loin cloth. Not the best attire for his first brush with the devil nettle!

He got it on his arms, chest, stomach and legs. 'It was itchy painful,' he recalls. Hives erupted, and to alleviate the pain he dove into a pool. It became doubly horrendous and he jumped out again. That night he shivered uncontrollably. By the next morning the hives had become depressions and the affected area was constantly clammy. For the following six months, any contact with water was enough to set off the 'itchy pain' again.

In the mid 1990s we were working in Vellimalai in the Periyar Tiger Reserve. On one of our treks looking for reptiles, our young friend Gerry spotted a skink and dove headlong after it. Rom warned him not to move while he yanked the nettle out of the way, but it was too late. Gerry had already brushed against it.

Two days later, accident-prone Gerry slipped off a fallen log right into a whole bed of devil nettles. His ears, neck, arms and legs were afire with the screaming itches. Surprisingly, despite the severity of exposure, the worst of the effects didn't last longer than 10 days.

Around 1820, the French botanist Jean Baptiste Leschenault de la Tour compared the pain induced by the nettle to 'rubbing my fingers with hot iron'. He also suffered contraction of jaw muscles so severe that he feared he had tetanus. It's not clear what toxin the plant injects to cause such severe reactions. Formic acid, serotonin, histamine, oxalic acid, tartaric acid are some of the suspects.

Col Richard Henry Beddome, however, didn't find the symptoms so extreme. It's possible that the irritation varies with seasons or perhaps some people are allergic to it. Despite the terror it arouses, there is still so little known about this weed.

Recently, when Rom and Gerry were walking in Agumbe they came upon a whole host of devil nettles and they both said their hair stood on end. The plant was so memorably traumatic they seemed to viscerally sense its presence. The two of them backed away quietly as if they had seen a ghost.

I asked Ramchandrappa, a botanical authority who works for the Forest Department in Agumbe, about this plant. He called it *'Malai Murugan'* in Kannada and said the antidote is lime juice or turmeric powder smeared on the affected areas. Apparently the symptoms subside immediately. Turmeric powder will be a definite addition to my jungle apothecary.

The Greatest Reptile Show
on Earth

What would the National Reptile Breeders' Expo look like? I struggled hard to imagine what kind of people would buy and sell reptiles. Maybe 'weird people' – pot smoking, long-haired, and elaborately tattooed dudes who rode Harley Davidsons. Rom, who had been to one such expo several years ago, shook his head, 'You've never seen anything like it.'

In August 2005, on a balmy Saturday morning, as we walked past the long queue waiting to get inside the convention centre in Daytona, Florida, I was amazed that 'straight people' outnumbered the weirdos. There were elderly people, young couples, teenagers, little kids. You'd think they were going to the supermarket!

The previous year, I had published a book called *Snakes of India: The Field Guide* by Rom and Ashok Captain, and I hoped to sell a lot of copies at the expo. As we wheeled cartons of boxes into the building, US Fish and Wildlife Service agents checked to see if I had any live creatures. If I had, I'd have to show a licence to sell them.

Strangely, my table was in the venomous reptiles section where adjacent tables were piled high with Gila monsters, black Pakistani cobras, albino rattlers, mambas, tarantulas and scorpions, all alive and dangerous. Everyone who visited this section had to show proof of their adulthood, just as they would on entering a bar. When sales were slow, I gawked at people examining venomous creatures in plastic see-through containers. Flanking me were Charles, an on-duty Florida State Fire Rescue Officer to handle emergencies, and our German buddy, Andreas Gumprecht who was selling his gorgeous book, *Asian Pit Vipers*.

At lunch, Rom took my place at the table while I wandered around the 600 odd stalls. There were the occasional jewellery and book stalls, but most of the floor space was taken up by live animals. There were womas from Australia, brilliant colour morphs of geckos, and crazily patterned ball pythons from Africa, orange garter snakes, bearded dragons, various tortoises – more reptiles than I had seen in any zoo anywhere in the world.

On the second afternoon, Charles rushed over bursting with news. He had just bought a baby king cobra for $350. He already had a pair of adults at home.

'Do you have space for another one?' I asked.

'Not yet. I'll figure it out eventually,' he replied, unfazed by his new commitment.

I was hung up on the large gorgeous South American tarantulas. They seemed more like toys than living venomous predators.

I had mixed feelings about this whole enterprise. It is no accident that Florida has an increasing problem of foreign animals colonizing its wetlands, including large reptiles such as Burmese pythons and Nile monitor lizards. Irresponsible owners had dumped unwanted pets that had outgrown their interests and apartments into the closest wild habitat. Andreas countered that it was keeping snakes as a child that honed his skill as a snake breeder. He kept 300 snakes of 50 species, so many that he had to rent a flat just for his creatures. And today he is one of the world's experts on Asian pit vipers.

In 2008, we were back at the expo to raise money for gharial conservation. The expo was now restricted to captive-bred, non-venomous animals. The quiet-natured and beautiful ball pythons had taken over; no other species was sold in as many numbers.

By the end of the weekend, thanks to an enthusiastic group of associates, we had raised close to $25,000 for gharial conservation from the sale of t-shirts, books, various items donated by individuals, zoos and organizations. The reptile fanciers' commitment for the gharial in far-off India was touching. I wondered if we could raise this kind of money for reptile conservation (do I hear an 'ugh'?) here, in middle-class India. Sadly, not a chance.

Birds Too Many

Every October, for about two and a half decades, flocks of egrets arrived at the Crocodile Bank and roosted in the trees overhanging the crocodile ponds. By day, they rooted around the rice fields and backwaters; in the evening, should we be Croc Bank bound, we would see formations of birds headed towards the safe airspace above the crocs. Occasionally some failed to return, having fallen victim to the ancient muzzle-loaders of the Korava tribesmen.

By December, the trees were covered in guano – a white Christmas. Come April, the birds forsook the Crocodile Bank for other places. Rom figured that the birds didn't nest here because the trees were young. To encourage appropriate thoughts of procreation, he tied woven bamboo baskets high up in the canopy, but the birds were not smitten with them. Eventually the baskets came floating down with the wind.

About 10 years ago, something clicked in the egrets' heads. They stayed through summer and began nesting. Within a couple of years, the population of birds at the Croc Bank increased exponentially. They were nesting all over the place, and not just above the croc ponds. Walking to the office from the kitchen was a game of roulette – the odds of being shat upon rising as the days went by. The worst days were when air-borne spoiled eggs, dislodged by parent birds, landed on one's head.

The raucous noise of parental squabbling and chicks' incessant pleas to be fed were deafening. To add to our woes, cormorants, night herons, and pond herons also joined the nesting orgy. There wasn't a single tree branch free of bird nests. On the weekly off-days, fully fledged chicks wandered the pathways like tourists, or posed like garden ornaments on the enclosure walls. Every morning the Croc Bank's clean-up squad had to clear bird droppings, regurgitated fish that the chicks had clumsily thrown up, and dead chicks, before the place could be open to the public.

The ones to bear the brunt of this avian assault were the tortoises. The beautiful colours and patterns of the Travancore and star tortoises were transformed to a uniform snowy white. One couldn't tell what kind of tortoise they were. Every week, they had to be bathed and cleaned of all the bird goo and I don't know which they hated more – the smelly scats that caked their shells or the cleaning. We worried that the animals might get some disease (bird flu maybe?) from this surfeit of guano.

When the late ornithologist, Ravi Sankaran visited, we moaned about our 'bird problem' and the menace of aerial 'bombing'. He protested that a heronry of this density was quite rare and we ought to protect it.

I joked, 'Yeah right, Madras Crocodile Bank and Bird Sanctuary!'

He shot back, 'Why not? If you built treetop platforms and set up scopes, bird watchers will visit in droves.'

Rom built on the idea, 'We could provide disposable ponchos with every ticket so people don't get upset by the droppings.'

These remained mere daytime reveries.

Then a wandering monkey showed up out of nowhere, and all hell broke loose. He stole chicks from their nests, tucked them under his armpits, and hobbled around clumsily. The parent birds shrieked and pecked at this intruder, but the monkey just swatted them away. Some chicks fell from his grasp and were eaten by the waiting crocs below. The staff tried to chase the monkey away. When their efforts failed, they complained to the authorities who didn't respond. The staff tried to trap the monkey but couldn't. Then just as suddenly the animal vanished. A few weeks later, a booted eagle arrived at what can only be described as a smorgasbord, but there is no sign of a dent in the water bird population yet.

Sometimes I tease Rom about his bamboo basket invitation to the birds when I want to make a point about good intentioned conservationists, and an embarrassed Rom begs, 'Don't even remind me, please!'

Run-ins with Snakes

One afternoon, the three orphaned mongoose pups I was rearing disappeared into a small bush behind the house. I could hear growling and snarling, and then suddenly a loud pressure cooker hiss – Russell's viper! I yelled, whistled and tried to cajole the pups back, but they were disobedient brats. I could see nothing, neither snake nor mongooses. All I could do was wait and hope for the best. Eventually, the threesome emerged unscathed, while the snake had apparently pushed off to a more peaceful abode.

When we first moved into the farm, there was more land than we could manage. Initially we carved a small garden around the house. The rest of the farm was left untended as we hoped native trees would regenerate from seeds dispersed by birds. Instead, weeds thrived and formed an impenetrable tangled mess. We couldn't have created a better snake habitat. The forest on one side and the rice fields on the other makes this farm a busy snake highway.

A few years later, our German shepherd, Malam died of suspected cobra bite. The experience shook me up completely, and I went brush-cutting with a vengeance. No matter how clean we kept the farm, there was just no avoiding the vipers and 'hooded death'.

Then we got Pokhiri Raja, an exceptional mongrel. As in the case of all the other puppies we have had, we allowed a watersnake to bite Pokhiri's nose. He yelped in pain while stumbling backwards, and he looked at the snake with renewed respect. Usually that was enough to train dogs to stay away from snakes forever. But Pokhiri took it a step further, and became so sensitive that he could literally smell snakes.

In the midst of a boisterous game with fellow pups, he would suddenly wander off with his nose high in the air. If we were out of sight, he growled and bristled in a special manner that he reserved just for snakes. No matter what we were doing, in the middle of a phone conversation or entertaining guests, if we heard that special growl, we were out of the house in a trice. Pokhiri's record in finding the reptiles remains unbeaten by any of the many dogs we have known.

So what do we do once the snake is spotted? At first, we used to scoop up the venomous ones and release them in the adjacent forest. But research showed relocation caused severe problems for them, maybe even death. The best thing to do, we realized, was to keep escape routes clear so the reptile could find its own way out.

A lot of people titter about how petrified they are of snakes. When it comes to rat snakes, just gulp down your wimpiness, and learn to live with them as they discourage all other snakes from taking up residence. If you remove that snake, another snake will surely fill its niche and it just could be a cobra or a Russell's. Which one would you prefer?

When we moved to the farm, Rom and I were romantic minimalists; we didn't want any furniture so we slept on the floor for the first year. Until one day he was bitten by a centipede, right on his tender ear. It could have been a snake, we exclaimed to each other with hands covering our mouths in dawning realization. Duh! We promptly got a bed, and since then there have been no untoward incidents.

The plants, that several of you believe will keep snakes away, just do not exist. There is no other way of discouraging the creatures from taking up residence than keeping the farm, garden or yard mowed and clear of piles of firewood, rubble and junk. Needless to say, there are likely to be occasional wandering snakes, so there is no substitute for being alert.

When Roses are Green

In the early days of seeing each other, Rom politely requested that I 'kindly refrain from wearing' my favourite salwar kameez, the one with tiny red flowers on a rich green background. Just as I thought darkly, he's already telling me what to do, he explained, 'The reds are flashing too much. I can't even look in your direction.' His colour-blindness sounded more like a psychedelic trip than a genetic mutation.

When the flame-of-the-forest trees are in full bloom, he can't see them until I point them out. If it's a solitary flower like the glory lily, then I have to describe its shape and location. Strangely, he can see red after it is pointed out; it appears to be a question of recognition.

Once when Rom was on a trip to the US, I asked him to buy me a jacket. I guess my expression soured when I saw the gaudy green colour. Rom asked innocently, 'Isn't it grey?' On the other hand, he was reluctant to wear a grey shirt I had bought him because he thought it was pink. I wish he was a painter so he could depict how he saw the landscape.

Doris, Rom's Ma, told me what a mistake it was to allow

her two colour-blind sons to drive her around northern New York State during the fall. Everyone else speechlessly marvelled at the wonderful mosaic of warm colours across the landscape, occasionally gasping 'ooh' or 'aah'. Before long Rom and Neel would exaggeratedly mime, 'OOH', 'AAHHH, what gorgeous colours!' and then look at each other and collapse helplessly with laughter. To them, the entire landscape was a monotonous dull brown.

On the flip side, Rom finds those green and brown snakes faster than anyone else I know. That's because he trusts shapes, not colours. Then he's the one who describes the vine snake or fer-de-lance and its location before I can see it. My colour-vision fools me when snakes are well-camouflaged. Call me shape-blind.

About 10 years ago, we were travelling through Rajasthan and arrived at a remote village after a hot, dusty drive. We were shown to a large, colourful tent where several turbaned elders were gathered around in a circle. A couple of men had come across the Pakistan border with beautifully made swords wrapped in velvet which the rest were taking turns examining very closely. As soon as we were seated, one of them offered us a gooseberry-sized sticky ball and pointed to a large earthen pot set in the middle. We were to tuck the opium ball in our cheeks and slowly sip buttermilk from the pot. While I politely declined, Rom was never one to refuse such an opportunity. I kept a watch on him out of the corner of my eye, half expecting him to keel over any minute. But he seemed surprisingly normal as did all the other venerable old chaps in that tent; opium seemed as casual as *paan*. The negotiation was long and tedious; time slid backwards and when it hovered somewhere in the 16th century, a deal on the swords was struck.

A couple of hours later, on our way back to Jaisalmer, Rom commented that he was able to see women's red saris. Long after the buzz wore off, he was like a child who had learnt a new trick. 'Red,' 'pink,' 'orange,' he rattled as he pointed to various colourful flowers, clothes and signboards, and he was right every time. I wish I had been able to access the tests to diagnose colour-blindness then. About 72 hours later, the effects wore off.

Rom believes his brief colour-vision was due to the opium, but it seems illogical that a drug can nullify a mutation in his X chromosome. But if I argue that scientists are still working on gene therapy as a cure, Rom mischievously suggests that more experiments are needed to prove him right!

The Ultimate Common-Sense Test

Over the years I've heard so many stories of people going completely berserk when they encounter snakes. Some snakes are venomous and pose a danger to humans, and therefore many people are pathologically afraid of these reptiles. But neither the fear nor the danger explains the lack of common sense some folk exhibit. I'm mystified by people's disproportionate reaction to these mostly benign creatures.

In the early 1990s, a newspaper reported this case from Florida. A man spotted a rattlesnake while he was mowing his lawn. I can almost imagine his villainous laugh when he decided to run over the poor snake. The blades chopped the snake to pieces, leaving a bloody mess. But the severed head flew through the air, and the twitching muscles caused the snake's jaws to clamp onto the man's cheek. He barely survived the severe envenomation.

The numerous Indian goddess movies get the general premise right – do evil and pay the price. But some people just don't seem to get it. Several years ago, we were travelling through the wet forests of Karnataka looking for king cobras.

We stopped at a tea estate where Rom had caught one in the 1970s. The estate manager and his wife were gracious hosts, thrusting homemade cookies and cakes on us, so we were forced to nod in sympathy at the tale they narrated. It seems funny on hindsight, but at that time, we were appalled and sad.

The manager had been away from home when his wife spotted a king cobra atop a giant silver oak tree near the gatepost. If she had let the snake be, it would have eventually gone away. Instead she had become hysterical and ordered the workers to bring the tree down. The snake then sought shelter by climbing another tree, so that one was hacked down as well. The harassed creature then escaped into the garage. She set the garage on fire and very nearly burnt the house down as well. As the injured king cobra slithered out, the manager arrived on the scene with his shotgun and dispatched it.

Firearms and snakes, like guns and booze, usually don't go well together. While out in the woods, an Iranian hunter came upon a snake, and the report wasn't clear if he was trying to catch or kill it. He used the butt of his rifle to pin the snake's head. As most snake people will tell you, when you do that the tail feels around seeking a purchase. In this case, it accidentally found the trigger, and shot the hunter fatally in the head.

As people slalom down the waterways of South Carolina in their motor boats, watersnakes (and occasionally a venomous moccasin) basking on overhanging branches dive into the water in fright. Sometimes they land in the boats. Panicky fishermen have been known to shoot the hapless snakes, sinking their boats in the process.

This one wins the award for stupidity. In Mississippi, a man saw a snake crawling along his garage and took a shot at it with his double-barrelled shotgun. Unfortunately for him, just behind the snake was a whole box of dynamite. The explosion killed the reptile and the man, and completely destroyed the building.

It's not only while killing snakes that people destroy property, get hurt or even killed. Take the case of these two amateur snake-fanciers in South Africa. They saw a stiletto snake, a truly unique snake. If you are stupid enough to hold its neck, its fangs open like switchblades outwards through the side of its mouth, and the snake strikes backwards into your hand. It doesn't even need to open its mouth to bite. One of the men picked it up and promptly got bitten seven times. Calling the bitten man a sissy, his friend proceeded to pick up the snake. And of course, he got bitten too. Both men survived after a sojourn in hospital.

What is it about snakes that brings out stupidity in humans? If people are so afraid, shouldn't they run away from the snake? Why mess with the creatures, and inadvertently inflict more pain, and even death, on themselves?

The most sensible thing anyone, who doesn't know snakes, can do is simply admire them and leave them alone.

Kings of Cool

We heard of *The Big Lebowski* for the first time in 2003, when visiting English friends took the mickey out of Rom by calling him 'The Dude', after Jeff Bridges' title role in the movie. Although made in 1998, we had not heard of the movie, and it was just then belatedly attaining cult status globally. Then a few years later, a British TV critic reviewing one of Rom's documentaries called him 'The Dude' and slowly the epithet began gaining currency.

Now a lot more people comment that Rom's cool, unflappable attitude towards snakes reminds them of The Dude. But little do they know that all of Rom's snake-hunting buddies – the brothers Heyward and Teddy Clamp, Winston Brown, Chockalingam and other Irula tribal pals, even youthful Gerry Martin – are as cool. After spending time with these veterans, I'm only slightly amused when younger snake-catchers and TV presenters tremble with hysteric excitement when faced with a venomous snake. I just don't understand what the fuss is about.

The coolest dude amongst Rom's snake-hunting buddies is Attila Beke. A Hungarian by birth, he had spent most of his life in the US. His English is still accented which makes even his most prosaic pronouncements sound exotic. Back in the 1960s, Rom and his friends were part-time commercial snake-hunters. Attila was the only one to make his living entirely by catching snakes and that gave him an edge; he developed that special skill of finding them with the least effort.

Rom recalls how they'd cruise along the back roads around Miami with Attila at the wheel. Attila would suddenly brake, lazily gesture to a discarded truck tyre lying off the road, and instruct Rom that if he ran his hand along the inside, he may find a king snake. Sure enough, it would turn out just as predicted, or even better, there might be two snakes!

Another time when they were riding along a bumpy dirt road lined with tall old casuarina trees, Attila slowed down and told Rom that there was a tree hole about 30 feet up, an easy climb, he claimed, just big enough to get your hand into, and the odds were that there would be one of those gorgeous red rat snakes inside. What turned out to be a death-defying climb was rewarded with one of the beauties. Rom could never fathom how Attila did it. Attila was the super cool snake dude, the one who knew just about everything there was to know about snakes in Florida.

A few years ago we met Attila at Heyward's Serpentarium at Edisto Island in South Carolina. Amongst the stories of recent snake related events was one about a young woman who had been bitten by a venomous copperhead at the local cemetery. 'Why was she there after dark?' Heyward wondered. No response except broad grins. 'Who is coming?' he asked and all of us chorused, 'Me!'

That fine moonlit evening we went copperhead hunting.

Except Attila, the rest of us wore jeans and sneakers. Attila was in his frayed cut-off jeans and flip-flops – no fancy snake catching gear for him. With snake hooks ready, Heyward and Rom walked ahead chatting and scanning the broad, neatly cropped lawn while Attila followed sedately. When the latter did come upon a copperhead, he pinned its head with his flip-flop! Picking up the snake's body with the other hand, he held up the handsome but snappy snake for us to quietly admire before carefully depositing it into a white cotton pillow case. Few people outside the snake community know of Attila, which is a shame.

The other day, Rom and I were both doing our kitchen chores with music for accompaniment when the sappy 1970s rock song 'Take it easy' came up. I couldn't help mimicking an exasperated Jeff Bridges, 'I hate the effin' Eagles, man!' Rom is beginning to so completely identify with the character that he quickly skipped tracks. The Dude abides!

Watchers at the Pond

Watchers at the Pond, a little known book, is a true classic in nature writing – as much a lesson on nature as about writing. It chronicles a year in the lives of various creatures that live around a Canadian pond. No cougars or large mammals sully the story; it's all about the littler creatures – from microscopic amoeba, earthworms, ants and wasps to a red-tailed hawk. Franklin Russell writes in a simple luminous style that got me so caught up in the drama of life and death through changing seasons that the book was unputdownable.

We were staying at the newly-built tree house overlooking the reservoir at Parambikulam Wildlife Sanctuary when I got hooked by Russell. I didn't want to go anywhere; just stay put and read. On one of those walks in the forest where I played truant, Rom suddenly encountered a sloth bear and ducked behind a bush. He said the bear was also startled, barked loudly, and darted behind the same bush. After a moment, Rom slowly peered around and found the bear doing the same. Eventually, both of them backed off slowly from each other.

Meanwhile, I was a nondescript little creature struggling beneath the ice – 'no great relief came from the suffocation crisis since the ice sealed the pond firmly against its own banks.' Caught in this vortex of depleting oxygen, I came up for air when water 'appeared in the pond at disparate points as tiny bubbles, which began reviving a few of the suffocating creatures.' Lost in this pond drama, I barely even registered Rom's close encounter.

Eventually I did tear myself away long enough to go for a drive in a thunderstorm. As lightning cracked open the skies and rain came down in a flood, we found a bedraggled jungle rooster sheltering beneath a solitary, broad teak leaf. As the jeep ground through the mud, we came across a herd of elephants and stopped to watch. Another lightning bolt crashed, and a squealing calf tried unsuccessfully to scramble under his mamma's belly. He was too big! I remember Russell's line:

> The lightning burned through the air and created a huge vacuum, into which the vapor-packed air hurtled. As this air smashed into itself from all sides, it created an explosion that rocked the earth, and the concussion fled along the line of the lightning strike and ended with a crackle far beyond the marsh.

There is little I can find about Franklin Russell online. The preface says he was a New Zealander working in Canada as a freelance writer, and that this book was the outcome of a suggestion made by the editor of *MacLean's* magazine. Russell chose a park in Hamilton, Ontario, to make observations for his assignment. He also visited other ponds in the swampy lowlands, surrounded by thick forests of oak, beech and hemlock. He spent days scrutinizing microscopic life in a laboratory and immersed himself researching in the library. The book is packed full of fascinating little details. 'In one summer, the trees would release more water than was contained in the pond.' And his writing grabbed you with its poetry. 'The pond had burst open like an expansive blossom and had seeded and died and was now settling and rotting back into itself.'

Brought up in a city, I was so far removed from life in the raw that I sought to find justice, cause and resolution to death. In reality it is 'quick, bright, forgettable', Russell writes. Death occurs because there was once life; something has to die to feed the living. The eternal dance of life and death drives not just plants and animals but even stars.

This is an out-of-print treasure available on used book sites, although who would sell their copies is beyond my comprehension. Like some endangered species, there is a whole trove of such priceless books slowly fading from human memory.

Snakebite

For centuries, huge numbers of people have died of snakebite in India. In recent decades, there have been several attempts to quantify 'huge numbers'. Unless we have these figures, there is no way to assess whether the problem is increasing or decreasing, and which areas are more prone to snakebite so something can be done about it.

Joseph Fayrer reported that 19,060 Indians succumbed to snakebite in 1880. After a year-long campaign of snake extermination (4,67,744 snakes were killed for rewards), he reported a marginal decrease: 18,610 people died. But in 1889, the number had shot up to 22,480 deaths when India's estimated human population was 250 million.

In 1954, Swaroop and Grab put together the World Health Organization's (WHO) first global snakebite estimates. They lacked real data from India and quoted a mere 20,000 deaths. Were they simply using the 1889 figures? In 1972, two Japanese researchers, Sawai and Homma took a crack at the problem. They visited numerous hospitals around the country, did some extrapolation, and came up with 10,000 deaths per year with the caveat that 90 per cent of the victims never approached a hospital.

Then in 1998, Chippaux estimated that snakes killed between 9,900 and 21,600 people when our population was on the threshold of hitting one billion. In 2005, WHO estimated 50,000 Indians died of snakebite, but in a study it funded in 2008, the fatality was pegged at only 11,000. That same year, the Government of India jumped into the number-crunching fray and came up with, ahem, 1,400 mortalities! Apparently six of the worst affected states never sent their death toll figures.

These estimates don't tell us much about the nature of the problem – has it worsened or become better? So far there has been a little bit of science, but in the face of a huge logistical challenge, numbers were extrapolated to arrive at wildly unstable estimates. Sort of like our wildlife census data.

A part of the problem is that snakebite is not a 'notifiable disease', that is, the Central Government's Health Ministry has not issued a data collection directive to the states as is the case with AIDS. The other problem is, of course, the obdurate belief in country medicine and quacks rather than antivenom serum.

Recently Rom took part in a major study to provide the first credible figures ever for India. Codenamed 'The Million Death Study', it overcame the problems mentioned above by using a method called 'verbal autopsy'. Family members of the dead were interviewed exhaustively, and the symptoms they described were analysed by three doctors to arrive at a cause of death.

The results of the study, published in April 2011, provided some astounding figures. Annually, there are a million cases of snakebite in India, and of these, close to 50,000 succumb.

When you look around the countryside, where most bites occur, and notice people's habits and lifestyles, these figures aren't surprising. People walk barefoot without a torch at night when they are most likely to step on a foraging venomous snake. We encourage rodents by disposing waste food out in the open, or by storing food grain in the house. Attracted by the smell of rats, snakes enter houses. When they crawl over sleeping humans on the floor who twitch or roll over, they may bite in defence.

Once bitten, we don't rush to the hospital; instead we seek out the nearest con man, tie tourniquets, eat vile-tasting herbal chutneys, apply poultices or spurious stones, cut-slice-suck the bitten spot, and adopt other ghastly time-consuming, deadly 'remedies'. As Rom cattily remarks, 'If the snake hasn't injected enough venom, even popping an aspirin could save your life.' That's the key – snakes inject venom voluntarily and we have no way of knowing if it has injected venom, and if it is a lethal dose.

The only first aid is to immobilize the bitten limb like you would a fracture, and get to a hospital for antivenom serum without wasting time. If every snakebite victim did that, there's hope of bringing down those horrendous mortality figures.

Frognapped! – A Frog's Adventure in the City

I woke with a rude shock and was petrified by what was happening around me. My whole world was rushing by so fast that I hung on with all the stickiness that my toes allowed. Everything was a blur. It was so disconcerting that I shut my eyes tight. The air stank; particles of black muck settled on me clogging the pores of my skin. My delicate toes almost fried in the heat, and my eardrums just couldn't handle the noise. Finally, after a lifetime, when the world came to a standstill, I was so numb that I very nearly fell down from dizziness. I was just gathering my wits when a voice yelled, 'Hey Rom, there's a tree frog here. What to do?'

The man called Rom answered, 'Just put him over there by the bushes.'

She was mortified, 'Here! At the mechanic's? He'll die.'

Rom tried to reassure her, 'No, no. He'll be fine.'

Was he nuts? How could I survive in this hot tinderbox of a concrete jungle?

She hissed, 'Give me that plastic bag.'

He questioned, 'What are you going to do?'

Just as I was about to make good my escape from their evil clutches, she caught me with the bag. She sprinkled some water from her bottle, threw some green leaves and knotted the bag tight. She bit a small hole in the bag and tucked me into her knapsack. That was how I came to be frognapped.

Although she kept the bag out of the sun in the autorickshaw, it was stifling hot and the air was unbreathable. But at least this bumpy ride was better than being poised a metre above the road that was zipping by at 80 kmph. On the way, Rom declared that I was sure to die before they returned home, and she was equally certain that she wouldn't let me.

After they had breakfast, she opened my bag and blew a lungful of air tinged with fumes of coffee. I gagged and spluttered. Rom teased, 'Is he still alive?' I caught her looking daggers at him as she tucked me back into the knapsack. By now the air conditioner of the restaurant had soothed my frayed nerves and I was almost all right. I even managed to dose off for a while.

After lunch, she blew some more air into the bag; this time her breath stank of raw onions. I would be fine but for her awful 'kiss of life'. How did the breath of the princess who kissed the toad-who-turned-into-a-prince smell?

Hours later, Rom took me out of the knapsack and set the bag down on a seat in a temperature-controlled vehicle. When was this nightmare going to end? Will I ever see my home again?

After a long time, I woke up to see her peering down at me. The bag was open! Seizing the opportunity, I leapt out blindly and landed on the nearest tree. She exclaimed, 'He looks perfectly normal. No sign of dessication.' I leapt further out of her reach. I looked around; I couldn't believe my luck. I was back in my regular beat. Home!

Later that evening when I narrated my adventures, none of my frog pals would believe me. By then, I could scarcely believe the story myself and was almost convinced that I had had a vivid nightmare. For one thing, which living creature could survive the heat, the noxious air and noise of that hell hole called a city? Did such places really exist?

I'm now being plagued by nightmares at my usual roosting spot. What if my world suddenly began moving when I go to sleep? What if I wasn't as lucky as the last time? I think I'll follow the advice of friends I met during the last monsoon and move to that huge, multi-roomed cave called a house. Those frogs had bragged that there was plenty of water, glowing lights at night that attracted lots of insects, numerous places to hide, and hardly any of those blasted snakes or birds. Tonight I'm moving in!

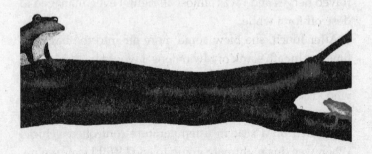

Gardening a Forest

My search for people working on tropical dry evergreen forests (TDEF) led me to the Auroville Botanical Garden. Started 10 years ago by Walter Gastmans, Auronevi Pingel and Paul Blanchflower, it is a 50-acre man-made forest comprising 250 species and growing.

With a degree in Forest Ecology from Scotland, Paul is the garden's full-time director. When they first started work, thousands of self-propagated *Acacia auriculiformis*, an Australian species, covered the land. They cut down most of the trees, leaving just enough to provide shelter for the native saplings planted amongst them. As Paul points out, this is a forest that regenerates in the shade and most of its nutrients are locked in the canopy. So if the forest is gone and the soil is poor, considerable investment has to be made to ensure that native saplings survive. The Australian acacia works wonders by not only enriching the soil with nitrogen, but also providing a suitable microclimate for the native trees to flourish. Once the saplings take hold and reach a certain height, the acacias are taken out.

Auroville is a massive seed bank of TDEF species. During the early years of planting trees, several Aurovillians travelled to tiny patches of remnant forests and sacred groves for seed collection. These seeds have grown into trees, cross-pollinated with individuals from other forests, and the genetic diversity of the resulting seeds is probably richer in Auroville now than elsewhere. So when the Botanical Garden was to be established, Paul didn't have to go far to find seeds.

Besides being a repository of native trees, the garden is also a large open-air classroom for school children. They spend the day exploring a labyrinth (check it out on Google Earth), learn how plants cope with the lack of water at the cactus garden, and discover that grasses provide 50 per cent of our nutrients besides roofing and other construction materials. Paul also plans to start propagating native species as houseplants that require little water and remain green even in the dry season.

I asked Paul what he saw as the future of TDEF – was it destined to hang on in tiny pockets, no longer in touch with compatriots in other parts of the range? He recalled his visit to the 300-acre TVS factory in Hosur which he is landscaping. About 30 per cent of the land area is set aside for vegetation and 10 per cent for water bodies, which has attracted a large number of painted storks and other migrants. Bullet wood and other deciduous trees have already been planted, and Paul has plans to plant native fruit trees to attract more birds.

Generally most afforestation programmes have used hard seeds as they are more resilient to heat and are viable for a long time. Seeds of forest fruit trees are not only more difficult to collect but also to germinate; their oils attract insects that bore into them. Although they pose a propagation challenge, they attract and support numerous species of birds and animals.

Other landscaping projects include the Hyatt in Chennai, where Paul is experimenting with a mixed species hedge. He declares that although he's not a 'TDEF extremist,' he tries to create a relationship between local varieties of plants and his clients. When he started work on Mahindra Resort, south of Puducherry, they weren't particular about TDEF, but now after winning environmental awards, the company has begun championing the conservation of a very rare forest type.

Since visiting the Botanical Garden, I'm thinking of ridding my garden of water-guzzling exotic houseplants and replacing them with local species. And I would urge you to do the same – try to source local saplings and plants rather than foreigners like the raintree and the gulmohar.

Tales from El Paso

During the Vietnam War, Rom was drafted into the US Army and was stationed in El Paso, Texas. His salary was $200 a month, but he needed to earn more to buy his ticket home to India once he got out. So he began hunting snakes on the weekends for zoos like Staten Island Zoo, New York. He also sourced East Coast creatures like red rat snakes and Florida king snakes from his friend, Heyward Clamp for the El Paso Zoo.

Rom was returning from the Huachuca Mountains after a weekend of snake-hunting when the cops flagged him down on the highway. A multi-state police alert had been issued, ordering him to report to the El Paso airport immediately. When he arrived, he saw a plane being systematically searched by the fire department. A box of snakes, sent from South Carolina to Rom, had broken open in transit. The authorities had found three bags with live snakes but also 10 empty ones. They were frantically going over the plane to find the escapees. Rom pointed out, 'Yes, the bags may be empty but they're folded. You think the snakes would fold them up before escaping?' The authorities didn't take kindly to the irony and admonished, 'This is a very serious offence, son. Make sure this doesn't happen again.' Heyward's mother had kindly sent a bunch of snake bags, with triple stitched seams, and these had been the cause of consternation.

Although Rom was a lab technician in the army, he was allowed to work after-hours at a private blood plasma collection lab run by a retired army man called Colonel Smiley to earn extra money. The war machinery had a huge operation to collect human blood plasma to make gamma globulin injections against hepatitis, a big debilitator on the Vietnam front lines. Blood drawn into bags was centrifuged so all the cells dropped to the bottom, while the clear plasma remained on top. The latter was skimmed off, the blood cells reconstituted with normal sterile saline, and given back to the donor.

On one occasion, Rom arrived for work at the private lab with a bunch of safely-bagged snakes, but there was no place to stash them. Keeping them in the car was not an option as it could get very hot. So he stuck the big brown shopping bag behind the building, way up on top of an air conditioner. Later in the evening, a policeman barged into the lab and began yelling about some snakes.

A shocked Rom scrambled outside to see all the snakes lying dead on the ground, and a Mexican woman hysterically shouting and screaming that Rom had almost killed her. The woman had tried to steal the bag, and when the writhing snakes still secure in their bags started rattling, she had panicked. She and others in the neighbourhood had shot and beaten the poor animals to death, then pulled off the rattles as souvenirs before calling the cops. Rom was so angry that he was ready to fight, but was held back by the cop. He never made the mistake of leaving snakes untended in a public place again.

After his incarceration in the army got over, Rom left El Paso for Florida, a two-day drive, in an unheated 1956 Ford in winter. It took a whole day just to drive across Texas. While he could bundle up and keep warm, he was concerned about his two pets, a Gila monster and a bull snake. They travelled on his lap, tucked under his overcoat, for warmth. There was one worry however – that the gila would latch on to a vulnerable part of his body. But it never warmed up enough to cause any harm. After leaving his pets with his buddy, Heyward, Rom caught a Greek freighter home, to Bombay; it took 53 days, but that's another story.

Jaws iii

Jaws was one of four saltwater crocodile hatchlings imported from Singapore by the Central Leather Research Institute, Madras, back in the early 1970s. The organization planned to slaughter them after five years to assess the feasibility of crocodile farming.

In 1973, when Rom's surveys showed that wild crocs were almost gone, he wanted to start breeding crocodiles at the Madras Snake Park. He went to the Leather Institute to have a look at the reptiles. As Rom and his Irula friend, Rajamani walked around the murky pond, one of the three-foot salties suddenly erupted out of the water and grabbed Rajamani's leg. It didn't bite deep or hard, but it took the two men by surprise. This was their first encounter with the species, and they realized it was a very different croc from the easy-going mugger they were used to.

Rom proposed to the institute's director that he would rear the salties and provide all the measurements annually in return for custody of the animals. The director thought it was a great idea; the expense of rearing the crocs would be the Snake Park's, and the animals didn't have to be killed. Eventually those four salties came to the Croc Bank.

When they reached adolescence, one began outstripping the others in size. Using his larger size to his advantage, he beat up the others everyday. In one of these skirmishes, he lost a part of his tail but gained a name: Jaws III.

Rom built five ponds in the same enclosure and visually barricaded each from the other. But no, Jaws was having none of that. He chased the others out of all five ponds. During the heat of the day, he'd have a choice of water bodies, while the others had to skulk on land in the shade. By this time, Jaws had reached 10 feet, and the others were still lagging at under seven feet. Clearly, he was the champion of the litter and had to be given his own enclosure.

For all his possessiveness about space, Jaws was a sitting duck when a vicious visitor thrust a sharpened stick into his eye, blinding him while he lay basking next to the enclosure wall. The staff couldn't find the miscreant.

Rom has always wanted to breed Jaws and propogate his 'giant genes'. One afternoon, in 1996, I sat in one corner of Jaws' enclosure filming a nine-foot femaie saltie being introduced. As the unsuspecting croc walked towards the pond, Jaws' 15-foot torpedo-body flew out of the water. He grabbed her by the middle and shook her like a ragdoll. When he tossed her onto the bank, the crew took her out of the enclosure before Jaws attacked again.

A few years later, Jaws' enclosure was divided in half, and another female saltie was introduced. They could see and smell each other through the gaps in the fence, but he could do her no harm. During the course of the following year, they were often found eyeballing and bubbling at each other across the barrier. The prognosis was good. But when the fence was removed, Jaws was back to domestic violence; he chased her right out of the pond. Over the years other unsuccessful attempts were made, and today we are all resigned to Jaws remaining celibate for the rest of his life.

Dealing with such a large animal can be awkwardly dangerous. Once, Jaws had to be moved to a bigger enclosure. After his ropes were untied, everyone was to jump off at the same time on the count of three. Rom began counting, 'One . . .' and his nervous crew immediately leapt off the reptile's back leaving Rom alone, straddling Jaws' shoulders. Feeling the weight on him lighten, the croc moved forward and Rom fell back. Thankfully, the animal was only interested in getting into the water.

Today at 16 feet plus and weighing between 500 and 600 kilos, Jaws is the largest croc in captivity in India.

Everything's in the Name

What do the smew, green mango, pewee, fieldfare, brambling, brown trembler, firewood gatherer, buffalo weaver, and green-tailed trainbearer have in common? They are all names of birds. Bird lists around the world are littered with plenty more bizarre ones – various tyrants (pygmy-tyrant, cattle-tyrant, tit-tyrant), the titmouse, kinglet, morepork, wandering tattler, bananaquit (besides orangequit and grassquit), monotonous lark, zigzag heron, familiar chat and sombre chat.

There is probably a reason for the strange common names of birds. For example, the bufflehead (a blend of 'buffalo' and 'head') is a duck with a large head. Bobolink (a group of them is called a 'chain'), killdeer, chuck-will's-widow and whippoorwill are named for the sound of their calls. The cloud-scraping cisticola flies so high that it seems to skim the sky, while the mealy parrot gets its name from the fine dusting of white resembling flour on its back. The limpkin, a rail-like bird, is named for its limping walk. Steamer ducks of South America are flightless, and when they need to get away fast, they flap their wings while paddling their feet like a paddle steamer. And 'screamers'?

Well, they scream. As a young teenager, I remember tittering about the 'tits'. I recently discovered that it's an old Germanic word for 'small' and these are tiny birds.

I also ran into a whole lot of bird names whose origins are murky such as bearded mountaineer (a hummingbird), jacky winter (a flycatcher), leaf-love (an African bulbul), powerful woodpecker (more powerful than other woodpeckers?) and festive parrot (it doesn't seem any more colourful than the others).

Many years ago, I was trying to teach Rom's brother, Neel, the names of various water birds at a large lotus-choked pond in Sri Lanka – coot, purple moorhen, whistling teal, pheasant-tailed jacana and so on. After spending half a day at it, he knew most of them. That evening when Rom came to pick us up, I was so proud of Neel's new-found knowledge that I preened.

'What's that one called?' I asked pointing to a white-breasted water hen.

He deadpanned, 'Double-breasted seersucker' (a formal Western light summer suit for men)!

In hindsight, I had to laugh at the ridiculous names of both birds and clothing. Just in case you are interested, 'seersucker' originated from the Persian word, *shir-o-shakar* (milk and sugar), which apparently described the material's texture – alternate stripes of smoothness and crinkliness.

Recently, Gopi Sundar, a biologist, acquainted me with the yellow-bellied sapsucker which left me gasping with laughter. He explained that it drilled little holes in tree trunks and licked the sap, and therefore its name was quite descriptive. Just as I was about to jettison my favourite rebuke, 'cross-eyed bow-legged buzzard' in favour of 'yellow-bellied sapsucker', Gopi innocently followed it up with another, the red-cockaded woodpecker! This was even better. As I tried it out for vehemence and stress, Rom cautioned me to never use it in the US.

Woodpecker is a slur against poor white rural people in the Deep South. The African Americans saw themselves as sweet singing blackbirds and Whites as noisy, irritating, and sometimes sporting red-heads like the woodpeckers. Over the course of time, the slur word became inverted to 'peckerwood', perhaps to mask its meaning. It has also been suggested that in some parts of Appalachia, peckerwood is the regular name for the bird. However, in recent years, it has been appropriated by some white supremacists in California, whose emblem bears a striking resemblance to the cartoon character, Woody Woodpecker.

Although it was too bad about the woodpecker, there is no dearth of bird names that can double as cuss words. 'Motmot' sounds appropriate for smiting one's head. It's easy to exclaim 'Chaco chachalaca!' in surprise, and 'matata', as a dire warning. Otherwise, *hakuna matata*! No worries!

Innocence Lost

About 20 years ago, inspired by Laurens van der Post's *The Lost World of the Kalahari*, I asked the Irula elders about their creation myths, songs and stories. No matter how grey their hair, I was given the same answer – they had none. Rom tried to soften my disappointment saying he had had no success either.

The Dude recalled that in the 1980s he came upon Doraisamy, an elderly Irula goatherd, standing by an enormous dolmen (a Megalithic funerary stone marker) in Chengalpattu. Rom enquired if his presence by the rock arrangement had any significance. The Irula pointed to his goats and calmly answered, 'My goats are grazing there.' Not to be dissuaded, Rom asked if his parents had told him any stories about the archaeological feature. The elderly man denied any knowledge, and then suddenly paused as if remembering something important. Rom eagerly leaned forward and the goatherd, pointing to the crack in the rock, continued, 'They said never to crawl underneath; it might fall.'

Laurens van der Post, however, had no trouble sourcing stories. I chuckled as I read that a Bushman in love carves a tiny three-inch long bow from the bone of a gemsbok, and makes arrows out of the rigid stems of riverine grass. Armed with these, he stalks the lady of his heart, and shoots a tiny little grass stem into her bare butt. He would have to be a foot away for such a minute arrow to reach its mark and stick. If she suffers the piercing, he knows he has succeeded; if she breaks it off immediately, it's heartache for him. Could this be the source of the iconographic bow-and-arrows carried by the God of Love, whether Kamadeva of India, Cupid of ancient Rome, or Eros of ancient Greece?

The book chronicles the expedition van der Post led into the Kalahari Desert in 1955 to seek out the San Bushman for a BBC documentary series. After numerous setbacks, the team arrived at the spiritual heart of Bushman territory, the Tsodilo Hills, near the Okavango Delta of present-day Botswana. Reading the book early in my career, as well as witnessing Rom's own respect for the Irula people, made a deep impression.

At a time when other authors, usually hunters, were consciously patronizing in their attitude towards natives, van der Post put himself at the feet of the tribals, holding them in reverence as his teachers. In lyrical prose, the author says that the worldview of the Bushman was 'never just the knowledge of a consumer of food'. Instead they knew the animals and plants, the rocks and the stones of Africa 'as they have never been known since'.

Few people in the world today conform to the Bushman's ascetic lack of possessions, 'a loin strap, a skin blanket and a leather satchel. There was nothing that they could not assemble in one minute, wrap in their blankets and carry on their shoulders for a journey of a thousand miles.' Even when we go on short trips, our suitcases are still heavy enough that they need to be rolled on wheels. Some professional travellers do emulate the Bushman's carry-very-little-austerity and blog about it in great detail, but most readers still shake their heads in disbelief.

Today, when some champion the removal of local people from forests, I'm reminded of van der Post's words: 'We other races went through Africa [read India] like locusts devouring and stripping the land for what we could get out of it. The Bushman was there solely because he belonged to it.' There is a need to set aside forests for the sole purpose of wildlife conservation, but the challenge is to do it with empathy and without causing further hardship to already marginalized people.

Snakes in Transit

So you have caught the most gorgeous king cobra in Agumbe and you need to get it to the Snake Park in Madras, a distance of 600 kms. How do you do it? In the late 60s and early 70s, when having one's own vehicle was a luxury, you had few choices – taxi (exorbitantly expensive), motorbike (snake could over-heat and die besides making you bow-legged and butt-sore), or public transport.

Rom secured the 12-foot long venomous snake in a cotton snake bag and packed it inside a woven bamboo basket commonly used to carry vegetables. It was a hot afternoon, and the entire railway compartment was asleep after a heavy lunch. At some point, Rom woke up to roll over and saw the wide-eyed look of amazement on a little boy sitting across from him. And he was instantly awake. The kid was staring at the basket that had been tucked under Rom's berth. The king cobra had burst open the seams of the gunnysack covering the basket and was pushing its way through. The head and neck were already out, but it was still in the snake bag and no threat to anyone. Rom tapped its nose and it immediately withdrew into the basket. He mimed 'shush' not to alert anyone and explained that it was a puppy. Still mute from the astonishing spectacle, the boy agreed in slow motion. Fortunately that warning tap was enough to keep the snake quiet until they arrived at the park.

This is by far the most dramatic story of snakes in transit. In the early 1970s, there was an animal dealer in Madras, TAS India, who bought kraits from the Irula tribals. He would then sell the snakes to the Haffkine Institute in Bombay for venom production. One such tribal woman, Velliammal had a window seat on a crowded bus and was cradling a bag of kraits, the most venomous land snakes in Asia.

When the bus rolled down Mount Road approaching Spencer's, Velliammal noticed a krait coming out of the bag. Freshly caught snakes will frequently bite the bag, and in the case of venomous snakes, the venom they spew corrodes the cotton fabric over time creating weak spots. The krait must have found one such spot and pushed to its advantage. She quickly jammed it back into the bag and was promptly bitten. The brave lady kept her cool and continued to sit tight, holding the hole closed; none of the passengers were even aware of her predicament. At Spencer's, she alighted and told the TAS boss that she had been bitten. After securing the snake in another bag, he rushed her to Royapettah Hospital for antivenom serum and she lived to tell her harrowing tale.

Around the same time, Rom used to frequent Baruipur. It was quite a distance outside Calcutta, not in the suburbs as it is now. He bought monocellate cobras, banded kraits, and spectacled cobras from this village of snake-catchers. Although it was known to be a rough place, Rom said he wasn't scared – 'Having snakes was like having a loaded pistol.' However, once he was accosted by a few thugs in a neighbouring village. When they realized that all he had was Rs 100, their attention shifted to the bag. 'What's in the bag, some *maal*?' they asked. 'Snakes,' replied Rom. They laughed dismissively and started to put their hands inside the bag despite Rom's protests. Just then, one of the cobras hissed sharply, and they realized that their quarry wasn't joking and left him alone.

These days, of course, there is no need to transport snakes across such long distances. It's much more fun to take their pictures and leave them where they are. Besides, now the law has a few things to say about such activities.

The Snake Guru

As a schoolboy in India, Rom had dreamt of visiting the Miami Serpentarium, a facility run by the legendary snake man, William 'Bill' Haast. Finally in 1963, when he was 20, he stopped by and was promptly offered a job.

This was the first opportunity Rom had of working with many venomous species. The arrival of a new shipment was always a cause for excitement. One memorable shipment came from C.J.P. Ionides, called 'Iodine' by locals, a famous African herpetologist in Tanzania. It was a tin can, like our old kerosene containers, that had been soldered shut on top and labelled with big, black formidable lettering: 'Beware Black Mamba'. As soon as the canister was opened, out popped the mamba; it had not been secured in a bag. Rom remembers the feeling of awe as the mamba stood up three feet high and spread a thin hood. Haast tiptoed around it, the snake swivelled as it watched him, emerging from the tin can little by little. When it was fully out, it measured eight feet in length.

Haast was never one to display any emotion whatever the circumstance. For instance, on one occasion he opened a cage and before he could peer in, the resident green mamba shot out and bit him on the thigh. Two little dots of red quickly appeared on his white slacks. But he remained calm, caught the snake, extracted venom, and put it away in its box. There was no sense of panic or urgency, although internally, he may have been cursing himself. To Rom, it seemed like an agonizing delay in getting to the hospital, which had been alerted of a possible emergency. Haast waited for symptoms to manifest, but it was a dry bite (no venom had been injected). So he continued with the work on hand.

For decades, Haast has been immunizing himself to elapid (like cobras, kraits and coral snakes) venom by regularly injecting a very dilute cocktail of venoms. The process is called mithridatization after King Mithridates VI of ancient Turkey who was apparently the first to try it.

In 1965, when a South American kid was bitten by a coral snake, for which there was no antivenom serum, the US government mounted a dramatic goodwill rescue effort. Traffic outside the serpentarium was blocked to land a chopper to take Haast to the Homestead Air Force Base. A waiting jet fighter then flew him to Venezuela, where the boy was battling death. Since Haast's blood was compatible, they gave a direct blood transfusion, and it is said, this saved the victim's life. This was one of the 21 snakebite victims he reportedly saved with his 'antivenom-blood'.

Rom worked for Haast for two years before being drafted into the army during the Vietnam War.

In the mid-1990s, we visited Bill Haast and his wife Nancy at their farm in Florida. Bill's hands were deformed from numerous snakebites, and I watched nervously as he pinned delicate little coral snakes by the neck to extract their venom.

Otherwise the 87-year-old was enviously agile, leaping over the five-foot-high wall around his eastern diamondback enclosure. Rom and Nancy reminisced over the old days, especially the time when he took her snake-hunting without Bill's knowledge and had to pay hell on their return. Neither of them heard Bill mutter good-humouredly, 'I remember that.'

Arguably the most snakebitten man in the world, Bill was 100 when he died in June 2011.

'Bill was the second major influence in my life, next to my mother,' Rom said as he blinked furiously that day. I was startled; I have never in our years together suspected that Haast could have been such an important figure in Rom's life. 'He was always meticulous, taciturn, not given to hyperbole or flamboyance. The most important thing was to get the job done. Always. I absorbed a lot of that. Maybe not to the same degree. . . .' His voice trailed.

The Venom Milkers

It was Harry Miller, the Welsh journalist living in Madras, who introduced the snake-hunting Irula tribals to Rom. The latter was so impressed with their abilities that he moved from Bombay to Madras so he could work with them, selling venomous snakes to the Haffkine Institute in Bombay.

Soon Rom figured that merely catching and sending snakes didn't bring much income. He had wholly supported the shutting down of the unsustainable snake skin industry which now left many Irula with no livelihood. Something needed to be done quickly and he was certain that selling snakes was not the way.

Rom conferred with his Irula buddies, 'Sure Man' Natesan, 'Eli Karadi' Rajamani, 'Nak Bulti' Vellai, and Raman, and suggested that since he knew how the venom milking business worked, having been trained by none other than the famous Bill Haast, they could set it up themselves. While the others thought it was a good idea, Sure Man joked that in this son-besotted country, a snake temple with real snakes would make more money than venom. Women who prayed at termite mounds for a son would flock to a temple with visible, live snakes, he declared.

The chief conservator of forests of Tamil Nadu felt the venom business was a good job opportunity for former poachers and suggested setting up a cooperative rather than a private company as the chances of getting the necessary permits from the government would be smoother. In 1978, a cooperative to be owned and operated by the Irula was formed with Rom as the technical adviser.

Rom then went to meet the state honchos at the Secretariat armed with a proposal for the Irula to catch a thousand snakes a year, keep them for four weeks for milking, after which they would be released. Four years of protracted negotiations later, the Government of Tamil Nadu issued the order allowing the cooperative to capture, milk and release snakes – but with 25 accompanying strictures.

The next big challenge was housing the numerous snakes. The Haffkine Institute used cumbersome metal boxes with mesh roofs and the Miami Serpentarium used special plastic and fiberglass cases. Neither seemed practical for Madras conditions nor did the cooperative have much money to invest. Rom had seen the snake charmers of Bengal and Maharashtra hold their snakes in earthen pots and that became the ideal 'low cost housing'.

In the 1970s, most of the Irula were immobile; if they had to get anywhere they walked. No bicycles or public transport for them. You couldn't blame them – they were paranoid about being identified and getting kicked off buses for carrying snakes. They are a dark people with curly hair, and when armed with a crowbar, their tool of the trade, the Irula stick out from the rest of the population. As with many tribal people, the focus of the Irula's interaction with the world is to blend in as much as possible.

At the end of a long day of snake-hunting, we've had to wait until they washed up at a farmer's well, changed into polyester pants and shirts and emerged spiffy clean while we looked bedraggled and smelt rank.

How were these shy people going to bring their snakes to the Snake Park? Of course, a few had already taken the plunge into mainstream India, but the majority remained reluctant. Since this was the only way they could earn money, it finally pushed some more of them to take the adventurous step. They would bring snakes caught by four or five others by bus, but some still walked all the way from Tambaram to Guindy, a distance of almost 14 kms.

Once the Irula Snake-catchers Co-op started operating, the Irula came up with several rules such as no young snakes, no gravid females, and no injured, sick or weak ones were to be brought. They had a good feeling for what snakes needed, and applied those principles in maintaining and transporting snakes. And that was how one of the most successful tribal cooperatives in the country came into existence. But Sure Man remained convinced till the end of his life that a snake temple would have been more profitable.

Creatures at Play

Every morning white-capped babblers swoop into the veranda to clean up the remains of the dogs' dinner. Then they alight on the roof and pick nocturnal moths and insects that had gone to sleep around the lights. The next foraging site is the garden where they flip over dry leaves looking for insects. When about 40 birds are so engaged, the dead leaves dance, fly and shuffle around. By mid-morning, they have swept through the garden without leaving a single leaf unturned, and they are sated. This is followed by a game – three or four run round and round a tree, chasing the one ahead. Sometimes the game gets very charged as they run up a tree trunk flapping their wings, crest the fork and then swoop down again on the other side. At this stage, the twittering gets so excited and loud that we forget about work to watch them.

I asked a bird expert if he knew of other birds that enjoy a game. He replied birds don't play, and they might be doing something else that appears like play to us. The more I watched the babblers' antics, the more convinced I became that they were indeed playing. What else could they be doing?

How do they all decide when to start playing? Among

dogs it is easy. They bow low with their rump in the air, wag their tails and grin from ear to ear. How can anyone resist such an invitation? There's a popular online video of a polar bear being similarly invited to a game by a husky. For a tense moment, it appears as if the bear is going to snack on the dog, but amazingly he recognizes the 'play bow' signal and the disparately sized animals play. The bear returned everyday for a week just to play with the husky. As for the babblers, I've yet to discover what cue gets them all going.

Dogs will do anything for a game. Specially-trained canines help biologists find scats of wildlife in Washington State. For instance, Gator sniffs out grizzly bear droppings, Ally specializes in wolves, and Tucker focuses on killer whale poop. They cheerfully set speed records for finding the most scats in the shortest time, not for an edible treat but for a 90-second game of fetch.

Zoo animals such as young female rhinos romp with barrels while lions, cougars, hippos and even turtles push, swat and kick balls. Belugas and dolphins blow bubbles from blowholes or mouths and frolic with them. I have no doubt that the drive to play is very strong in animals.

Villagers brought an orphaned rusty-spotted kitten, the world's smallest wild cat, to a Sri Lankan friend of ours, whose pet cat nursed it along with her offspring. During our visit, the wild cat was half-grown and bursting with energy. She chased a string with which I was teasing her through a hot summer afternoon until I was out of breath. She could effortlessly race up the seven-foot-high smooth front of a wooden cupboard after the twine. Two hours of such boisterous play later, I was exhausted and the kitten was still going strong. No cat I have known could play with such stamina, agility and imagination.

Why do they play? To me, that's a silly question. Why do we play? It relieves stress, builds camaraderie with our mates, improves motor control, and mostly, it is just sheer good fun. Biologists, who sometimes have to prove the obvious, are finding that it's the same with animals. Every evening, our dogs look forward to playing just as much as they eagerly anticipate food. They begin getting restless at 30 minutes to game time, reading my face for the slightest hint, jumping up every time I move, and rushing to the door if I get up. When animals and birds play, they are expressing a sense of well-being, their *joie de vivre*.

The Ethiopian Giants

A few years ago, Rom was chasing giant crocodiles around the world for a film. Strangely, the hot favourites of numerous wildlife films, the famous River Grumeti in Tanzania or River Mara in Kenya, where some truly impressive beasts waylay migrating wildebeest and zebra, didn't figure in his itinerary. Instead, there was one place we had never heard of before – Lake Chamo in Southern Ethiopia – that was said to have even bigger crocs. A licensed hunting safari operator reported that his clients had shot a few 18-footers in Chamo, and he had a hunch larger crocs were lurking.

On the very first day out on the lake, we saw congregations of these huge reptiles that were not in the least shy. More than the Nile crocodiles, we were wary of hippos; if we threatened them or came between mother and calf, our boat could be swamped by the momentum of a thousand-plus kilogrammes of muscle and blubber armed with four dangerously long canines. Unlucky people have been grievously bitten by these mammalian monsters.

The average size of the large crocs sunning themselves on the banks was about 14 to 16 feet. A few were 18-foot giants.

Day after day, we went out hoping to find that monster who would stretch the tape at 20 feet. But sadly we couldn't find any. Rom said the massive ones hardly ever basked on land; the large scales on their back acted like solar panels absorbing heat even as they swam with most of their bulky bodies submerged. So it was tricky business finding that ultimate behemoth.

To get away from the tedium of film-making, one afternoon I visited the nearby Arba Minch Croc Farm. At the entrance stood a large case of enormous crocodile skulls collecting dust and cobwebs. Using the spine of my notebook, I measured the biggest one through the glass. My jaw dropped. It was larger than the largest Nile crocodile skull on record.

Back at the hotel, I told Rom to visit the farm with such urgency that he may have expected those skulls to jump up and run away any minute. On a slow filming day, he finally decided to visit. I suspect he did it more to humour me than out of any hope of finding a jaw-dropper. I must confess I smirked when I saw him excitedly calling the manager to open the case so he could measure the skulls accurately. He looked up from his measuring and said it was possible that the largest was the head of a 20-footer; it's not very accurate to estimate total lengths of crocodiles from skull lengths alone. Sadly, this monster and the others nearly as big had drowned in simple fishing nets.

A year later, Rom returned to Ethiopia to assess the possibility of croc ranching as a local livelihood option for the numerous tribes living along the banks of the lake. He found it unacceptable that such huge animals should drown in fishing nets or that trophy hunting should selectively weed out the biggest and the best male crocodiles from the population. If he could draft a sustainable scheme by which the smaller sized crocs could be exploited, those large ones would have secure futures.

During the day, Rom interviewed the various tribal communities and at night, escorted by a nervous guard with an automatic rifle, he surveyed the lake for crocodiles. It was daunting to hear the hippos grunting in the dark, not knowing if one was about to attack or when the security guy would lose his nerve. Soon after Rom returned to India, trophy hunting of crocs was shut down. But before the ranching operation could be set up, the management of Ethiopia's parks changed and the Chamo giants may yet be doomed.

Dead Little Birds

Arunachal Pradesh may be technically a part of India, but culturally, it is so very different. On one of our first visits to the state, we drove all day through Nyishi tribal villages and settlements, meeting chieftains, shamans, and elders in full ethnic regalia. They were adorned with hornbill casques, goral horns, eagles' feet, racket-tailed drongo tail feathers, leopard jaws, and bear and primate fur. Throughout the entire trip, we were to see much more dead wildlife than live. We also noticed firearms and ammunition shops were almost as common as tea shops. One settlement didn't have a grocery store but boasted of a warehouse for arms.

Soon we saw our first hunter. A little Maruti 800 car was parked off the road and a well-dressed man stood beside it, pointing his rifle up into a young tree. As our vehicle whizzed past, we craned our necks to see what he was aiming at. Nothing more than a small bird could have hidden in that tiny canopy. As we climbed higher into the mountains, we not only saw little kids with catapults but also hunters armed with air rifles, .22s, and shotguns, with and without scopes. It was a disorienting experience. Were we in India?

When we were able to stop, we asked the hunters if they had bagged anything. They invariably replied they had been out for hours and had not found a single bird. Paradoxically, despite this hunting ethic, new species of birds, animals and little creatures are being discovered here.

Not wishing to jump to judgments, I spent a few hours on the phone after returning home, talking to friends working in the Northeast. Whether it was Arunachal, Nagaland or Mizoram, I heard the same thing. Hunting was a way of getting animal protein, ornaments as well as medicine. We did see some domestic pigs and chicken but not nearly enough to support the human population. Modern healthcare had not made any inroads into large parts of the region, and people still relied on cures procured from the wild. If Granny fell ill with fever, barbet soup was one cure.

Unless the conveniences of modern civilization reach such remote areas, any talk of conservation would be disconnected from their reality. Even if these needs were met, they would continue to hunt for the 'rush', said some hunters. It was their culture; it was in their blood. To our outsiders' eyes, advanced weapons, major hydroelectric dams, and a rising human population clearly threatened the survival of wildlife. Against this background, working with local communities, as ourornithologist friend, Ravi Sankaran was doing in Nagaland, will go further in protecting creatures. He felt that even achieving a reduction in the extent of hunting would help bring back wildlife, since so much of the forested lands are owned by the communities. The standard model of conservation – declaring protected forests and keeping them off-limits to hunters – isn't working here. For example, Namdapha is a large tiger reserve where no one's seen a tiger in recent years.

Months later, we were travelling to Arunachal again and stopped at Nameri, on the border with Assam, to meet Ravi. He narrated that on one of his field visits, he had run into a group of Mishmi hunters who were carrying the carcass of a takin. This is a large goat-antelope with a weird head, described as a bee-stung moose. When they were a day's march from the village, the men dispersed into the forest and returned a few hours later with lots of dead little birds. Startled, Ravi asked them why they went to that trouble when there was so much takin meat. They said that women were not allowed to eat takin but little birds were permitted. Ravi summed up his story, 'We conservationists have got our premises wrong, man. If they wanted their women to make them happy that night, they had to shoot those birds.'

Little Creature Discomforts

She had a puzzled look when she opened the door and caught me peering into the large cow bell hanging in front of her apartment before ringing it. We were meeting for the first time in ages and I had apparently just confirmed what she had heard through the grapevine – I had become weird. I didn't realize the significance of that look until recently.

To her credit, some months later, Kamala gamely came to stay at the farm for a few days and I was to catch *that* look several times. Finally, I asked her what was up. She said she thought I had developed some kind of phobia. Surprised, I challenged, 'Like what?' She replied, 'You just picked up that clean wok from the cupboard and washed it again before putting it on the fire.' 'It might have frog piss,' I explained and opened the corner cupboard wide to show her the menagerie of frogs happily squatting on pots and pans. The cabinet door didn't sit flush against the shelves, a carpentry defect that I call the 'frog flap'.

Following her rapid-fire burst of questions, I had to explain my actions.

- Tuck the ends of the bedspread touching the floor under the mattress to prevent unwelcome creatures like scorpions and centipedes from climbing up into bed with us.

- Vigorously shake clothes and towels that have been hanging on pegs overnight before wearing/ using them, just in case caterpillars, scorpions and centipedes are hiding in the folds.
- Knock shoes out before putting them on to avoid the unpleasant surprise of your toes meeting squishy toads or painful scorpions in the cramped space.
- Check the hinges of doors and windows before closing them so as not to flatten sleeping frogs and geckoes.
- Never pull out books by the top of the spine, a convenient scorpion hiding spot, and before replacing the books, check the gap for geckoes and their eggs.
- Remember to place a large piece of cardboard and close the potty's seat over it before going to bed. Frogs assume the potty is their own private perennial pond, and at midnight, I'm in no mood to argue.
- Look under cushions before sitting down; it's less hassle than cleaning squashed skinks and geckoes.
- After a long absence, inspect the bedding thoroughly for the nests of the long-tailed tree mouse.
- Check the inside of the washing machine and oven for frogs before using them.

I could go to great lengths sealing our open house and keep out all animals but that would be a truly weird thing to do in the tropics.

Kamala then pointed triumphantly to the calendar that displayed the wrong date and month. I sighed tiredly, 'Look behind it.' As if expecting a goblin to burst out, she lifted it gingerly and the many frogs that had been asleep leapt in different directions, pissing in fright. I explained, 'I ought to change it in the evening when the frogs are out hunting but I never remember, so the calendar stays out of date. You may as well change it now.'

Wide-eyed, Kamala wondered why I had peered under her cow bell. I dragged her out to show a similar cow bell I had hung in front of our door, thinking it was ethnically chic. She took one look at the wasp nest and its denizens buzzing actively inside the dome of the bell and jumped back in alarm. At least she didn't shriek.

After this long session of queries, I could see she was trying to answer her own questions when new situations presented themselves. When she saw me putting on my gloves that evening, she gave up, 'Now what's that for?' 'Have to rake the yard and I get blisters,' I replied with a big grin. Maybe I should have answered, 'It's time to wrangle the anaconda,' just for the reaction!

The Playful Porpentine

'It's like a pig with spikes,' said one. 'It has a face like a rabbit,' said another. We stood around the cage staring with curiosity at the captive young porcupine chewing on a piece of carrot. The poor creature had been confiscated from a small travelling circus and brought to our forest camp in Kerala.

Our team of wildlife nuts fed the spiky fellow kitchen waste and chicken bones, watching it chew, gnaw, and crunch with its rabbit-like front teeth. Its eyes closed blissfully while grinding into a bone. Reaching through the bars of the cage, we patted the bristle-covered head. Sometimes it would turn around and optimistically present its bum for a scratch. It was a cuddleable animal but for the armour of lethal quills.

To give the porcupine more space to exercise, we fabricated a large portable outdoor enclosure. Venturing inside for the first time, it bit every root, stem, and seed, sampling and tasting; everything must have been so new. Suddenly it became excited and rushed sidelong towards us, with its foot-long quills erect; we leapt over the low barrier in a hurry. For long, we had believed like Shakespeare that the 'quills upon the fretful porpentine' stood on end from fear. But apparently the animal erects its armour in play as well. Soon we were giggling as we ran around the enclosure with a playful, bristling porcupine hot on our heels. Once when Rom was too slow to react, one of the quills pierced his jeans and sank painfully into his calf.

As the porcupine walked, a bunch of short, hollow quills around the tail rattled. Everything this walking pincushion did was fascinating. None of us had observed such a wonderful creature at close quarters before. It had a few hours every evening in the enclosure as the fence wasn't sturdy enough to hold the animal overnight.

Days later, when we took the porcupine deep into the jungle and let it go, it came running back. We yelled, threw sticks and finally, it got the message and ran away. But when we turned to leave, it followed us. It was all getting too poignant, but eventually we chased it by raising a huge racket and quickly skedaddled before it found us again. That was nearly 20 years ago, when we stupidly believed that captive wild animals were hard-wired with the skills needed to survive in the forest.

For many days, we felt sad on seeing the empty cage. We imagined the porcupine was happy in the forest where it really belonged, but a small voice in our heads challenged that assumption. The porcupine, innocent of human hunters and predators, very likely fell prey to one of them. A friend commented that if it approached the first human it met, it would end up as a pot of 'thorny-pig' curry. Another said that surely by that time, it would have become wild and learned to avoid humans. There was a very slight chance that it survived, but we'll never know.

While releasing these wild creatures makes us feel good about having done a noble deed, they will most likely die, whether they are predators such tigers and leopards, or prey animals such as our porcupine. In the case of carnivores, there is an additional concern – since they don't fear people, they may attack and kill humans.

Despite some well-publicized cases and guidelines issued by the Ministry of Environment and Forests, six hand-reared leopards were let loose in Bandipur and Bhadra Tiger Reserves, Karnataka, in the year 2011. Three men were killed and three wounded by these animals. Two of these cats were killed by people and the forest department in self-defence, two trapped and, last heard, the other two are still at large. Releasing wild animals that are used to people is unacceptable for both the animals' welfare and local people's lives.

Mithun Rustlers

We paced back and forth. The window of good weather was short and we wanted to make the most of it before the rains swept in. We were in Papum Pare district of Arunachal Pradesh, a part of the country where we didn't know the language or cultural nuances. Finally, Nabum Radhe, our liaison man, arrived an hour late, muttering under his breath, his face twisted into a scowl.

Thieves had tried to steal his family's *mithun* in the middle of the night. The previous evening, Radhe's brother had gone looking for the free-ranging animals and found the calf wandering alone, crying in distress. Some distance away, he had found the mother tied to a tree, and he figured that it was the handiwork of thieves. After dark, armed with a rifle, the brother waited in ambush. At midnight, when two men came to take away the mithun, he shot at them but missed; they ran for their lives. With the thieves at large, the brother called Radhe for help. The latter let the air out of the tyres of the hired getaway truck and took away the keys.

Mithun are domesticated gaur, the largest wild cattle in the world, which they resemble a great deal. The former has short, symmetrical, outward-facing horns, a massive ridge on the back, white socks, rippling muscles, and smooth, satiny skin. On average, a bull mithun stands at 1.7 metres high and can weigh up to a tonne.

Here, in Nyishi territory, these animals play a central role in their cuisine, religion, and economy. A man's worth is measured by the number of mithun he owns. A calf costs Rs 20,000 and a cow can be more than Rs 40,000, said Radhe. Nyokhum, the annual Nyishi festival, is not complete without a ritual sacrifice of the bovines.

On our drive to Leporiang in April, we had passed a bridal procession carrying head-loads of pork, Pepsi (the Nyishi of this district drink gallons everyday), dried mithun meat and other goodies. While the men in our vehicle gawked at the pretty ladies in their tribal finery, I was smitten by the gorgeous mithun cows and a calf, the bridal price. They are the most handsome bovines in the world.

In our search for creepy-crawlies, we frequently encountered mithun grazing on the steep hill slopes. Despite their massive muscle-bound size, they are remarkably light on their feet, bounding up almost-vertical gradients. Radhe warned me against approaching the mithun because they could be dangerous. The animals are unused to people; they free-range through the forests and the owners check on them only occasionally. The bovines aren't marked or branded; most have unique blotches used to identify them. Disputes are sorted out by the tribal council.

That morning, after the cattle rustlers struck, Radhe's mind was not on the search for reptiles. By noon, we were exhausted and headed back to the village. Amazingly, the driver of the getaway truck from the previous night showed up and pleaded for the vehicle's keys. In exchange, Radhe demanded the mobile number of one of the rustlers. Later when he reached a spot with mobile connectivity, he found to his dismay that it was a fake number.

That evening, Radhe's brother identified the thief. Every family has a distinctive style of weaving rope; they still use natural fibre here. Examining the cord still tied to the mithun, he recognized the craftsmanship of his neighbour. That family's patriarch, unaware of his wayward son's deed, confirmed it. The tribal council would study the case and fine the thief. It's possible he would pay in mithun.

I'm still wondering how to bring a mithun or two home. A couple of Nyishi men had enquired about my bridal price. Their faces turned inscrutably blank when they found out Rom got me for free. My man's beginning to get worried when he catches me looking at him with a calculating glint in my eye.

Good Luck Talismans

Decades ago, when Rom was hunting snakes in the Western Ghats, he believed that the vibes of civilization interfered with his ability to find camouflaged reptiles. He took off his clothes, watch and the ring his father had given him. Clad only in a loincloth and with a hornbill feather shoved in his scraggly hair, he crept through the jungle and came upon his first wild king cobra. On separate occasions, a shepherd and a woodcutter fled on seeing this ghostly white apparition in the dark jungle, dropping their staffs, knives and axes. They must have wondered if they had set out at an inauspicious moment that day, while leeches and ticks would have thanked their lucky stars for the bare-bodied feast. Perfectly rational human beings like my man can become superstitious when they go hunting or fishing. They may take to wearing special beads, performing rituals, or chanting.

I'm not one to set store by good luck talismans. But two memorable incidents made me pause. A few years ago, I was invited by reptile professor, Harvey Lillywhite to Seahorse Key, an island off the West Coast of Florida. A huge nesting colony of water birds added life, noise, and a distinctive odour to the island. The messy chicks frequently puked up the fish their parents stuffed down their gullets. Waiting below were fat, venomous water moccasins that scavenged the stinky manna dropping from the trees. Snakes are predators, meaning they like to hunt and kill their own prey. But here, Harvey had discovered that moccasins would even swallow seaweed as long as it smelt of fish.

A few days previously, I had been gifted a pair of earrings made of gaboon viper fangs by Denisse Abreu, one of those rare women in the snake venom business. As I wore them that Florida evening, I wondered if the earrings would bring me luck.

At dusk, Prof Lillywhite and I walked along the forest edge looking for moccasins, taking great care not to spook the sleeping birds. It was one of *those* evenings when everything happened as if perfectly scripted. I saw males courting females, snakes foraging for half-rotten fish, and others coiled up like fat automobile tyres with their heads poised in the centre, ready to flash open their white mouths in warning should we approach any closer. I didn't want the night to end. Those delicate earrings were potent.

On another occasion, I was hiking up in the Santa Monica Mountains, outside Los Angeles, with my brother and his wife. As we were approaching the crest of a hill, my brother who was ahead exclaimed, 'Snake.' I rushed over just in time to see a beautiful red snake with black and white bands disappear into the bushes. Was it a harmless milk snake or a venomous coral? I couldn't tell and neither could the others. I memorized the sequence of colours – red, black, and white – to repeat it later to Rom.

A few minutes later, I stopped dead in my tracks. I realized an image of the snake we had just seen covered the front of my T-shirt. It advertised a popular reptile hobbyist's website, www.kingsnake.com. I was blown away by the freaky coincidence.

Later, I began describing to Rom all that had happened. He interrupted, 'There are no coral snakes in California.' When I mentioned that the snake was identical to the kingsnake.com logo, Rom got excited. 'I can't believe you saw a mountain king snake. A Californian mountain king snake!' 'Is it special?' 'Oh yes. It's a very rare 'un and one of the most beautiful snakes in the world. I can't believe it.'

I've worn the shirt and earrings on other snake-hunting trips but the spell had worn off. Maybe it works only on moccasins and king snakes. In the meantime, Rom thankfully has learnt the art of finding king cobras with his clothes on.

A Letter to IIT, Madras

Dear IIT-ians,

Living in a sprawling campus, adjacent to Guindy National Park, you have the best of both worlds – the advantages of living in a big city while escaping its worst irritations. But this luxury comes at a small price. A recently commissioned report on the management of monkeys in your campus says bonnet macaques are scaring some of you. Scaring? Is that all?

Apparently seven troops totalling 195 individuals hang around four hostels, the administration block, a residential area, an engineering block, nursery, and the garbage dump. Compared to wild areas, the report suggests, there may be too many monkeys and recommends moving three or four troops from the campus. While this is the commonest method of dealing with unwanted wildlife, it has no scientific validity nor is it humane. Besides, isn't it ironic these animals are unwelcome in a national park complex?

Translocated animals do not stay put where they are released; they wander far and wide, perhaps attempting to return home. Dr Rauf Ali, who studied bonnet macaques in Kalakkad-Mundanthurai Tiger Reserve says, 'Macaques translocated to the middle of forests invariably find their way to the nearest human habitation.'

I live in a village about 60 kms south of you and have dealt with translocated troops over the years. Let me tell you what is likely to happen to your monkeys after they are moved.

In short order, they will become agricultural pests. Desperate farmers will try to guard their fields but they cannot be vigilant all the time. When they cannot cope with the problem any longer, they will set off 'rocket' fire-crackers under the roosting trees at night and harass the terrified monkeys. If that doesn't scare the animals away towards the neighbouring settlement or if they get used to the fireworks, the monkeys will disappear, one by one, in sometimes gory ways. You may cry foul at these methods but these farmers are really at their wits' end. They don't have the clout to summon the local officials to deal with a situation they didn't create.

If monkeys are released so deep in the jungle that they cannot find their way to the nearest village, how are they going to survive? What to eat and what to avoid is learnt from watching others. If moved to a completely different habitat, your monkeys will be at a distinct disadvantage and many will die. As Dr Wolfgang Dittus, a primatologist of the Smithsonian Primate Biology Programme, who has studied macaques for the last 30 years says, 'Translocation of monkeys or any wildlife to a national park or wildlife refuge is a clear death sentence for the displaced – it is a political solution, not a biological one. It's a coward's way of killing the monkeys.'

After exporting your problem, are you likely to have

peace? Dr Ali says, 'New macaque troops will immediately move in to occupy the vacant spaces left by the ones that have been removed.' Nobody wins, neither you nor the monkeys. You would have only succeeded in spreading your problem to other places. Besides, it's the situation that is causing the trouble, not the animals.

People think monkeys are cute and funny when they feed them, but what are the animals thinking? In macaque hierarchy, it is the subordinates who willingly give up their food to dominant ones. So they begin to think of humans as subordinate macaques who can be bullied into submission, says Dr Dittus. Freely available garbage further compounds the problem. Designing monkey-proof garbage bins is surely no big challenge for your engineering students.

You live on the campus of one of the premier scientific institutions of the country, one carved from a wilderness area, which warrants some adjustments. I'm certain your technological skills and scientific understanding can find ways of adapting to life with bonnet macaques.

Sincerely,
Janaki Lenin

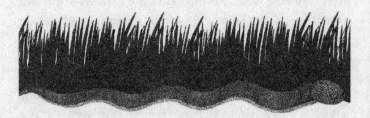

Catch Me a Barta

It's a snake that strikes fear in the hearts of everyone in Arunachal. Apparently scores of people die of its bite every year. One Nyishi said that the punishment for committing perjury in the name of the *barta* was death; the snake would seek you out and 'finish' you. There is no escape.

Stories like these spurred Kedar Bhide, a snake expert from Mumbai, on the trail of the barta. He was in the Northeast making a film on the gregarious flowering of bamboo in 2006 when he first heard about this dangerous reptile.

Some species of bamboo flower and seed simultaneously across their range, providing a feast for native rodents. The rats grow fat and multiply exponentially, attracting scores of predators, including the barta. The Nyishi stretched their arms as far as they could without wrenching their shoulders to show the length of the snake.

This is one of the least-explored parts of India and the chance of discovering a new species was high. Kedar doggedly followed every lead. Eventually, in a tiny hilltop settlement called Sangho, he found a couple of barta and identified them as Kaulback's pit viper. The species was first discovered in the late 1930s in Pangnamdim, Northern

Myanmar, by Col Ronald Kaulback after whom the snake was named. Until now, it was found in only one other place: Medog, Southern Tibet, China.

Rom wanted a venom sample from the snake to check its potency. In April 2011, six of us arrived at Leporiang, a valley at the end of the motorable road. Sangho was a distant hilltop shrouded in clouds and mist; at night not even a twinkling electric light gave away its location.

Early the second morning, a wizened old man arrived to say his son had killed a barta in the forest and thrust a woven bamboo bag at us. Rom upended it on the ground and a four-foot green snake with black markings fell out. This was our first look at the species.

An argument broke out among the Nyishi. Nabum Radhe, our liaison man, claimed it was a *taji* and not a barta. We had never heard of a taji before. What could it be? Radhe said the pattern on the head of a barta was different. In any case, the specimen was useless for extracting venom as it was half-rotten.

Identifying the snake was a tedious process – counting and examining the scales on the head, around the body, along the length of the belly. There was no doubt it was Kaulback's pit viper. Maybe the taji was just a variation of the barta. Radhe took umbrage. He claimed, the taji was small, non-lethal, and found in the forests of the foothills, whereas the barta was large, lethal, and found in the higher hills. Some pit vipers come in a bewildering array of colours and patterns, so it could well be that taji were young barta.

One day, when the rest of the team went hunting in a private forest which was reportedly crawling with the species, I hiked up to Sangho, the barta capital. Almost everyone was out working in the fields. A middle-aged Nyishi woman said she had never seen a barta. Her kinsmen had killed one last year, three the previous year. It was not at all common. Did it kill many people? No one had been bitten in Leporiang for the last 16 years. In Sangho, a young girl died of its bite about five years ago. Was this a case of hype being deadlier than the snake?

The team returned empty-handed. The bamboo didn't flower as profusely as expected and the dreaded rodent population explosion never occurred. Perhaps that may explain the lack of barta.

Although the next barta epidemic may not occur for several decades, no Nyishi will take a chance and commit perjury.

A Few Years of Solitude

Visitors from the city and the local village invariably ask, 'Aren't you scared of living alone?'

Taxi drivers dropping us home late at night get the jitters when we turn into our forested dirt road. Over the few minutes it takes to arrive at our gate, they repeatedly ask if there is indeed a house at the end of the lonely path. Some have been specific about what they fear – ghosts. 'Haven't seen one so far,' I reply and enquire, 'What do they look like?' Normally garrulous men turn silent as they focus on the road with great intensity. Once they drop us off at home, they just want to get out of here fast. They don't want tea or even water.

At night, our farm probably looks desolate to our visitors; not a single neighbouring house can be seen. The nearest village is a kilometre away, although new houses are popping up closer towards us. For now, we live in magnificent solitude. Over the years I've become addicted to it; any more than three days with people, and I get crotchety.

When I emerge from my bolthole once every few weeks, I need to consciously think my way through normal social interactions. The effort tires me out but it likely tires others even more. I don't feel the need to fill silences; in fact I don't even notice them. When Rom is travelling, the dogs and I live in companiable silence. Sometimes I comment out loud to the dogs about something I read. They are telepathic, they don't need a preamble. In response, they cock their ears to say, 'Is that so?' With Rom, however, I have to narrate the story from the beginning. What a long way he has to go.

Besides the occasional sound of traffic, cicadas and birds dominate the airwaves. One young chap from the city said in wonderment over lunch, 'I can hear myself chew.' This relative silence is what makes the festival season so unbearable when temple loudspeakers from the nearby village start up at unearthly hours. We read the Noise Pollution Act to the village headman at the start of every season and it has a marginal effect. Sometimes we play music to drown the scratchy songs that are on a repetitious loop, but mostly we just plug our ears for those few weeks and listen to our heartbeats instead.

The one disadvantage of this situation is that it's hard to get a village lady to come to work. They are scared to walk up the forest path alone even in broad daylight. They say people will suspect their morality. More than that, however, is the traditional negative view of the forest as an uncivilized place. People come to the forest to do what they dare not do at home – drink, meet their paramours, gamble and even murder.

Convinced by friends, Rom went to the extent of buying a burglar alarm but it was too much effort to fix. Besides, more than intruders, there's a greater possibility that passing wild animals would trigger the alarm. So instead he pulled out the motion-sensors and rigged it with a video camera so we could watch nocturnal wildlife.

A friend visiting from South Carolina asked me quietly at the end of his first day here, 'Do you have a gun?'

Startled, I countered, 'Why would I need one?'

'To protect yourself.'

Having thought long and hard about the security issue, all I can say is that our reputation as weirdoes who keep ghosts, snakes and other creepy-crawlies company is more of a deterrence than a firearm.

In any case, reading the papers makes me wonder if the city is a safer place. Neighbours within whispering distance of each other are oblivious to burglaries and murders. Perhaps I ought to be asking the question, 'Are you not scared of living alone in the city?'

Appearances are Deceptive

Born in New York and raised in India, Rom has made this country his home. He always felt Indian. When he went to the US briefly in the 1960s for an aborted college education, he had a hard time adjusting to life as a 'white American'.

After his return to India, he became hung up on the Andaman Islands, Indian territory then closed to foreigners. Using this opportunity to set 'right' his nationality, Rom traded in his American citizenship for the privilege of visiting the islands. Since then, he has had to constantly explain what a white man like him is doing with an Indian passport.

He is routinely interrogated by immigration officials of every country we visit – where he was born, who his parents are, why he holds an Indian passport. When so many Indians wave American, British, and passports of other nationalities, why is it so abnormal for an American to hold an Indian passport? Nevertheless, this anomaly has made some sticky situations more difficult.

One night, many years ago, Rom and I were cruising for snakes along the US-Mexican border. Snakes come onto roads at night to absorb warmth, and driving slowly is an easy way of hunting them. It was a deserted road and we were focused on finding snakes, when a siren went off behind us suddenly. It was the Border Patrol.

The officer was Hispanic, and he started rapping away in Spanish to me. I had to cut him short with 'no habla español.' He wanted to see proof of identity. 'India,' he drawled thoughtfully. And Rom? 'Also Indian.' The agent had never heard anything so weird in his life. A white Indian? His eyes darted from Rom's face to the passport and back. More questions followed. Finally, he had no choice but to be satisfied with Rom's Indian nationality. Then he asked where we were headed and why were we driving so slowly. Rom replied, 'We are looking for snakes.' He might as well have said, 'I am a Martian.' When I realized the officer was going to lose it, I nervously jabbered about the rattlers we had seen that evening such as Mojaves, western diamondbacks and black-tails. Eventually, he let us off. A couple of hours later, as we headed back slowly, a patrol car parked along a dark alley flashed its lights in greeting.

On another occasion, we were hunting sidewinder rattlers in California. About 20 miles west of Yuma, near the junction of California, Arizona and the Mexican state of Baja California, are the rolling Algodones Dunes. Around mid-morning, just when we called it quits for the day, a couple of choppers showed up and buzzed low, raising a sand storm. We struggled to keep our eyes and mouth clear of grit. The choppers moved away only after two ground patrol vehicles arrived. By this time, we were bedraggled, and a film of sand coated us head to toe. Annoyed at being harassed, I answered the officers' questions in sullen monosyllables. The poor officers thought they had busted an attempt at human trafficking. They looked at us like we were circus freaks and that restored my good humour.

Contrary to Rom's experiences, I have been unquestioningly adopted by diverse nationalities from Ethiopia to Indonesia. It all changed when I chopped off my shoulder-length hair. Everybody disowned me. Indians thought I was Malaysian, Malaysians probably thought I was from Timbuktu. Even people in my old neighbourhood in Chennai began speaking to me in English. On the positive side, what I lost in hair length, I made up in the language department. Although I've only been speaking Tamil since I could talk, I'm now complimented on how well I speak the language for a 'foreigner'. I now realize why Rom gets annoyed when he is treated as an outsider in his own land.

The Mite-y Peril

'Scrub typhus,' pronounced the doctor. 'What's that?' I asked. It is spread by the larval stage of a large number of trombiculid mite species. These tiny devils target small mammals, like rodents and birds, but accidentally get on humans.

Rom had just returned from Arunachal Pradesh complaining of a severe migraine-like headache and the shivers. I was convinced he had cerebral malaria but within hours of checking into emergency, he tested negative. Screening for dengue, leptospirosis and scrub typhus followed. By the time he tested positive for scrub typhus, he was talking gibberish, didn't recognize me nor was he aware of his name. An MRI indicated encephalitis and the fluid from his spinal cord tested positive for meningitis. Even as the doctors started him on antibiotics, I feared for his life. Those were dark days. Finally, five days of delirium later, Rom's condition took a turn for the better and in another 10 days, he was discharged.

Since the doctor insisted this was a disease of the 'deep jungle', I investigated further. 'Scrub' is a misnomer as the disease appears to occur in sandy, semi-arid, mountain deserts, rice fields, and even urban areas. In fact, *junglies* are not the only ones in danger of contracting the disease. A friend who lives on the beach, not far from us, contracted scrub typhus in her home of twenty-odd years.

The word 'typhus' comes from the Greek '*typhos*', meaning 'hazy,' referring to the state of mind of the patient. The villain of the piece is *Orientia tsutsugamushi* (in Japanese, '*tsutsuga*' means 'small and dangerous' and '*mushi*' means 'mite'), the parasite that causes scrub typhus. Written records of the disease date back to the 4th century in China and the early 1800s in Japan. Worrisome scientific reports say the disease is re-emerging in several countries, including India. Today, one billion people are exposed to the disease and one million are infected annually.

According to the World Health Organization's website, one can contract scrub typhus anywhere in the 'tsutsugamushi triangle' – from Pakistan in the west, to Japan in the east and the islands of Indonesia in the south. In mid-September 2011, scrub typhus outbreaks were reported in Nagaland and Himachal Pradesh. Three people died in the former and more than 13 in the latter.

In all these years of visiting jungles around the country, we've always dismissed leeches and ticks as minor irritations. Anyone who fussed about getting bitten by them was clearly a novice or a wimp, and we had no patience for his complaints. None mentioned mites, maybe because you can't see them. Before setting out for the jungle, if we remembered, we'd douse ourselves with insecticide. Ignorant of scrub typhus' long history of debilitating humans, we were more concerned about the negative influences of chemicals than about diseases.

During the Second World War, an estimated 36,000 soldiers were incapacitated due to or died of scrub typhus, a disease even more dreaded than malaria. One report said more troops were laid low by tsutsugamushi than direct wartime casualties. Between 1942 and 1946, the United States of America Typhus Commission made a major effort to prevent, control and treat the disease by using miticides, issuing insecticide impregnated uniforms, burning and clearing camp sites.

The Wellcome Foundation Laboratories in the UK produced a vaccine, and 2,68,000 cc was dispatched to India between June and December 1945 to inoculate Allied Forces serving in Southeast Asia. However, little is known of its efficacy and there is no vaccine currently available. In those pre-antibiotic days, mortality was as high as 50 per cent. According to one study, meningo-encephalitis was found in all cases of mortality from scrub typhus. Since then, antibiotics have saved many people's lives, including Rom's.

You bet, we are going to be dousing ourselves in insecticide containing DEET (short-form of N,N-Diethyl-meta-toluamide) before setting out for the jungle hereafter. Better to be a wimp than knock on heaven's door.

Look Before You Leap

I can remember only one instance when Rom let me walk ahead of him in a forest. That was more than a decade ago in Havelock, Andaman Islands. It was mid-morning when I came upon a green snake on the path and I exclaimed, 'Look!' Rom ordered urgently, 'Catch it.' But by that time, the snake had whizzed past. A few minutes later, there was another snake on the path and I couldn't help myself. 'Look,' I cried. An exasperated Rom demanded, 'Instead of saying "look", why can't you jump on it first? I can always "look" later.'

Leaping on snakes is not hardwired into my reflexes and I was defensive. 'Why do you have to go after every snake you see?' I demanded. 'Can't you just watch it? Do tiger people catch every tiger they see?' He replied, 'It's impossible to watch snakes like you would mammals. And the only way to identify the species is to catch and examine it.'

That's true. Many species of snakes look identical, while some species come in a range of colours and patterns. Hence herpetologists do not usually trust the looks of a snake. If anyone had the temerity to say, 'I saw a brown snake with bands,' the experts would retort disdainfully, 'There are so many; what's the scalation?'

During the early days of my association with Rom, I'd often step into his office and overhear a group of snake-people engaged deeply in conversation. This is how it would go.

'The pre-frontal is fused with the loreal.'

'Are the third and fourth supralabials touching the eye?'

'It has one anterior temporal.'

'What are the scale row counts?'

'17:17:15, 170 ventrals, anal divided, 50 subcaudals.'

It sounded vaguely like English. Eventually I learnt experts count the number of scales in a row, down the length of the belly, and examine their arrangement on the head in order to identify the species. No allowances are made to this hands-on approach to identification even when dealing with venomous species.

For instance, herpetologists cannot identify some species of pit vipers by looking at the scales alone. The only way to tell one from the other is by everting the hemipenis (snakes have two joined at the base) which looks like a sado-masochistic tool – covered in spines, bumps, cups, calyces, and folds. Or it may be boringly smooth. I fear for the sanity of the nerdy herpetologist who catches a female of one of these troublesome species. He may never be able to tell her apart from her cousin, and that's enough to drive him battier still.

In their efforts to classify and organize snake species, herpetologists will go to tortuous extremes. In June 1947, Angus Hutton, a 19-year-old tea planter working in the High Wavy Mountains of the Western Ghats, discovered two young grassy-green pit vipers wriggling their little red tails amongst the leaf litter. Some snakes use this trick to attract frogs and lizards. When the prey comes close, the vipers shoot out and sink their fangs. Two years later, Malcolm Smith, the father of Indian herpetology, described the two as a new species and named them after their discoverer. Since then, no other specimen of Hutton's pit viper has been found. This is unusual but not unheard of.

However, the really strange fact is that not only is this pit viper's closest relative found in Southeast Asia, it is identical to Wagler's pit viper in looks and scalation. We don't know what the hemipenis of Hutton's pit viper looks like as the specimen hasn't been dissected. The only distinguishing characteristic – the tail of one is longer than the other. Woe betide the herpetologist who finds one with a tail almost the same length as the related species.

I, for one, am convinced that the obsession with scales, hemipenes and tail lengths warrants classifying snake-people as a different species. Besides, I have caught one and examined him in fairly great detail.

Fencing with Porcupines

The two young trees on the farm were completely girdled. Removing the bark of a tree all the way around prevents vital nutrients from travelling between roots and shoots. I examined the teeth marks closely; it had to be porcupines. That's too bad, I thought, these trees are going to die.

When we first moved to the farm, porcupines were hard to see. If we saw a quill on the path, we were excited. Since then these rodents have made a big comeback. We began to see them regularly crossing paths, and our camera traps have caught them from every angle. They made big excavations around some trees and gnawed on their roots. This didn't seem to harm the trees in any way. We examined their poop closely – grass seeds, paddy, and compacted fibre. But they were clearly eating much more.

The porcupines dug tunnels under our fences, and helped themselves to the kitchen garden. On their way, they nibbled on trees. Over time, almost every tree in our garden began to bear tooth marks, but thankfully, the creatures didn't do a thorough job of girdling the trees. If we placed a monetary value on our plantation, porcupines would be our number one pest. But we didn't mind them. They were just an addition to all the creatures living off our farm.

A couple of years ago, on our evening walk, the dogs began straining at the leash. They wanted to go into an overgrown area of the farm and since we have a lot of snakes, I was reluctant to unleash them. With threats, treats and taps on their noses, I managed to get them into their kennel and returned to investigate.

A porcupine had been killed, neatly eviscerated, and its quills 'plucked'. Blowflies swarmed noisily over the pile of guts. The undergrowth was flattened where the kill had happened. Although I searched through the whole area, there were no other body parts – no head, paws, or skin – lying around. It seemed like the work of a cat, a large one. Who else could it be but our neighbourhood leopard? But wasn't eating a prickly creature like a porcupine dangerous? Didn't Jim Corbett narrate stories of tigers and leopards turning man-eaters after being debilitated by porcupine quills? I asked friends studying these cats if porcupines were part of their normal diet.

M.D. Madhusudan, an ecologist based in Mysore, said he had found dozens of tiger and leopard scats with porcupine quills and hair while working as a research assistant in the early 1990s. So it appeared that the resident prickly rodents were attracting large cats right into the farm. It should not have come as a surprise, but I did swallow hard when I realized that the cat may have walked past the house.

The next evening, as I walked the dogs near the 'kill' site, a movement in the distance caught my eye. Two half-grown porcupines scooted into the bamboo hedge. Was it their mother who got killed? Were they now orphaned? I kept watch for several days but saw no further sign of the young ones.

Last year, a tree planter from Himachal Pradesh enquired

if I knew how to deal with porcupines. I protect valued saplings with empty plastic bottles – cut off the top and bottom, slice one side open and slip it around the trunk. For larger trees, I build little fences to porcupine-standing-on-hind-legs height. But you can only do this for some trees, not an entire plantation. Perhaps encouraging leopards would solve the problem, I suggested half-seriously. He was aghast.

I wondered how North American tree planters handled their porcupine problems. This is what I found – recipes for porcupine stew and marinated porcupine chops. When our neighbour saw me fencing a tree, he had recommended something similar. His eyes glistened as he salivated, 'They taste just like pork.'

Monkey in the Middle

When we chat with neighbours, I see us from their perspective. The view is not very flattering. First of all, we were pretty hopeless at growing cereals. When they offered well-meaning advice on the use of artificial pesticides and fertilizers, we shook our heads. Instead we laboriously concocted degradable additives. For amateur farmers, the effort was too much and we didn't do it often enough. The pros watching our downhill slide to failure tried to convince us yet again to spray chemicals. We refused and the bugs took over.

After three or four years of such desultory farming, we gave up altogether. Instead we planted trees. From our neighbours' point of view, we were undoing decades of their forefathers' efforts to clear the land and make it suitable for farming.

'Are these trees medicinal?' they asked.

'No,' we replied.

'Then why do you plant them?'

'To prevent grass from growing.'

We spent lots of money every year keeping the grass low as it was a major fire hazard during the summer. We hoped the shade of the trees would prevent it from growing. Our neighbours, of course, had heard of nothing so daft. They stared at us in incomprehension.

They tried again, 'Why don't you get cows instead?'

'They need too much care and we are barely home.'

As the trees grew and integrated with the forest, monkeys used the canopy as an overpass to raid our neighbours' farms, mornings and evenings. They took a lot, and wasted even more. They even roosted in our trees. Neighbours recommended we set off 'atom-bomb' firecrackers that were so powerful they made the earth tremble. We balked. Like all naïve wildlife conservationists, we were namby-pamby, soft-hearted primates destined to lose the war against our 'lesser' cousins.

Then we made it even worse. Villagers here don't share our sense of privacy. Many times I've walked into the kitchen to find a goatherd filling up his stainless steel pot with water. I don't begrudge people the water, but it's disconcerting to suddenly find a stranger in the house. We planted a bamboo hedge. As it grew tall, our neighbours complained it sucked up all the water and nutrients from their rice paddies and nothing grew in its shade. As a compromise, we now keep the bamboo trimmed down to eye-level. This thick hedge became an ideal shelter for a host of other unwelcome creatures such as Russell's vipers, porcupines, and hares.

During the heat of the day when the farmers were sleeping off their heavy lunches, a peacock and his harem would swoop down and peck at the ripening heads of grain. At night, porcupines nibbled on their crops. During peanut season, jackals used our farm as their launching pad to dig and feast on the oil-rich nuts. We had brought the forest closer to the farmers.

When we didn't do anything about these pests, the neighbours thought we were queasy and offered to trap or shoot them. We demurred. After all, we could afford to be softies as we weren't making a living off our farm like they were.

The conflict with the villagers came to a head when a leopard colonized the forest and took one of our dogs. The villagers suggested that we use our superior interceding powers and get the Forest Department to relocate it. After having spent so many years preaching coexistence with wildlife, we had to face the ultimate test in our own front yard. We opted to make life more secure for our dogs while the big cat feasted on the villagers' goats and calves as they grazed in the forest. Despite their losses being greater in monetary value, amazingly, the villagers left the leopard alone.

In retrospect, for all the trouble we pose, I'm sure our neighbours would like nothing more than to trap and relocate us, the pesky conservationists. Yet, thankfully, they don't treat us like the monkeys, but tolerate us like they do

Son of a Wolf

'His name was Romulus, and his friends called him Rom.'
Rom blinked in disbelief when he read this first sentence.
The book was about the Khyber Pass in Pakistan and the
character, Romulus, was a British soldier fighting the
Pashtuns. Rom had picked up the novel from the officers'
mess on a Greek freighter en route to India from the US.

His name was so unusual that Rom had met only one
other person with that name outside the family. Rom's
father was Romulus Earl Whitaker Jr (but everyone called
him 'Earl') and his grandfather, Romulus Earl Whitaker Sr.

A few days ago, I wondered where the name Romulus
came from. Rom's parents divorced when he was a child
and his mother and siblings moved to India soon thereafter.
There was hardly any contact with the Whitaker family
except for the couple of times Rom met his father.

In response to my questions, Rom brought out a genealogy
that his stepmother, Bernice, had drawn up in 1991. His
father's family came from North Carolina and Virginia.
About four generations ago, there was a great-uncle called
Romulys Whitaker. Whitaker appeared to be a corruption
of Whitacre which derived from de Quitacre. It's not clear

how John de Quitacre who lived in the early 1300s suddenly came by the surname as there seem to have been none others before him. I flipped to the last page to find Rom's earliest ancestor was a person called Egbert who died in the year 839, more than a thousand years ago.

Who were these people, where did they live, and what did they do? I resorted to that ready reckoner, Google, and stumbled on several Whitakers who served in the Civil War, Second World War, and were listed in cemetery burial records. I began to laboriously match names with Rom's genealogy. There were many more misses than hits. Then I came upon a cousin's website which had a detailed genealogical record of the family. David Wooten's grandmother and Rom's grandfather were siblings.

In 1619, Jabez Whitaker left his family's 'The Holme' in Lancashire, England to arrive in Jamestown, Virginia where he purportedly built the first hospital on American soil. His brother, Alexander, is said to have converted and baptized Pocahontas, the famous daughter of an Algonquin Indian chief. The earliest Whitaker on record was Johias (1042-1066).

The further I traced the history, the more confusing it became, especially when 148 men and women crowded one generation alone. A lineage of knights turned into a cast of minor royalty – barons, earls, counts, and dukes. They were preceded by kings and queens from all over Europe.

In Roman mythology, Romulus and Remus, the founders of Rome, were suckled by a caring she-wolf. In reality, Rom is a descendant of one. Isabella Capet was called 'the she-wolf' by a contemporary writer for the beastly treatment of her husband, Edward Plantagenet, the First Prince of Wales. He was imprisoned at the Berkeley Castle and months later, gruesomely killed.

I expect church records show these familial connections. But then, history morphed into legend. I stared in disbelief when Greek mythological heroes like Priam and Aeneas rubbed shoulders with Biblical ones like King Solomon and Noah. And then came Venus aka Aphrodite, the Greco-Roman Goddess of love. Among the oldest characters in their shared genealogy, according to David Wooten, is Lamech, a sixth generation descendant of Cain, son of Adam.

Despite the interesting dramatis personae, my mind came circling back to one. Rom is apparently the progeny of Aeneas through his first wife, Creusa, while the original Romulus and Remus were descended from his second wife, Lavinia. Astonishingly, this makes Rom and his legendary namesake half-brothers, several times removed.

We don't know what prompted Rom's great-grandparents, Frederick Ann Whitaker and Caroline Winifred Stanly, to name their son, Romulus. However, when I now pronounce the name, it is potent with history, legend and symbolism.

Threats Bear Fruit

Before we could enjoy the fruits of our labour, before even the dratted monkeys could enjoy the fruits of our labour, our mango trees refused to flower. The horticultural department suggested enriching the soil with nitrogen or potassium, I forget which. We did as instructed and nothing happened.

Then a tree-planting friend suggested we might be watering our trees too much, so they were putting forth shoots instead of flowers. Withhold water, he said, and we did, not even yielding when the trees looked pathetic. No show. A few years passed and our mango trees burst into bloom. Then of course, our troubles with the monkeys began.

I've written off getting any fruits from the mango trees now. But when I realized that none of our animal friends like citrus, I planted a whole bunch of kumquat seedlings. Almost every one of them survived to adulthood. But no flowers. One website suggested exposing the roots. I didn't think that was advisable. Another suggested spraying *panchagavya* on the trees.

Every traditional farmer has his own favourite recipe for the mixture, but generally it contains the five products from a cow – dung, urine, ghee, milk, and curd. All these ingredients are mixed together in an earthen pot and set aside to ferment. This concoction is then diluted in water and sprayed on trees. Farmers swear it does wonders for plant growth, improves the soil, controls pests and induces flowering.

A dear friend shared her favourite panchagavya recipe. She added jaggery, over-ripe bananas, sugarcane juice, coconut and its water, and crushed bean sprouts. Enthusiastically, I got down to preparing this magic, albeit strong-smelling, potion.

Buying most of the ingredients was expensive but at least easy. The real challenge was getting the cow piss. I had to be at the neighbour's cow-shed early in the morning before the animals were driven off for grazing. Eventually, bespattered but triumphant, I returned home with a bucket of urine.

The trees have to be sprayed every 15-20 days and I ran out of stock. If you don't have cows, making this concoction is an involved process. I was too busy with other things to bother playing 'horticultural witch' again. So it was back to square one.

Someone said prune the trees, another said no. One said give them fertilizer, another said that would only make them grow. Contradictory advice meant I did nothing. And then a friend from Goa suggested I beat the trees and curse them loudly. 'You must be joking,' I exclaimed. He swore it worked; he had seen it with his own eyes.

On a recent visit to Yercaud, we met a couple who had an orchard. I asked, 'What do you do to make trees flower?' He went through the usual – watering and fertilizing. And then his demeanour became more serious and he suggested that when all else fails, I ought to beat and scold the tree.

A jack tree in his garden wasn't flowering for many years. One night, when his neighbours couldn't see him, he whacked the tree with an old broom while berating it for not flowering. 'You have to do it seriously, angrily. You cannot laugh,' he cautioned. 'And it worked,' he summed up triumphantly.

We heard the same story from Wynaad. This was not a local tale but pretty widespread. Clearly some trees need corporal punishment to make them behave well.

However, I'm not tempted to try this, whether night or day. It's not the neighbours I dread but Rom. He can always be counted on to reveal any embarrassing incident to friends, especially city ones who have no clue about country life. How can I keep up the pretense of being angry with the trees when Rom's laughter rings in my ears? Besides, he insists on calling my trees 'come-squats'. I imagined he would regale someone with, 'Then Janaki beat the come-squats. And guess what? They did diddly-squat.'

Animal Crazy

When we were wildlife documentary producers, we spent three months of the year in Bristol, England, editing the films. The nature of tropical natural history is such that our visits were always during the English autumn when the air had turned nippy and all sensible birds had fled to warm Southern countries.

We became starved for animal contact within a couple of weeks of arriving in Bristol. So acute was the need for such interaction that one afternoon, we watched a fly buzz drowsily against a sunlit window with the same level of interest that we would have shown a rare tropical insect. That's when I knew we had to do something before we went crazy.

We made occasional weekend trips around the country to go snake and lizard hunting with friends. One of those years, there was a major relocation of great crested newts in Petersborough. A brick company had dug up the soil and the resulting flooded ditches had been colonized by these amphibians. Now that the clay was spent, a large housing project was slated to come up on this vast man-made wetland. Since newts were a protected species, they had to be moved out of harm's way before the builders arrived.

Numerous volunteers and staff laboriously caught newts in buckets. Before the move to the new site, every newt had to be identified. The pattern on the amphibian's belly is unique to each individual and building a databank of identities would help in monitoring the animals in the future.

The photocopier stood out in the car park with its power chord sneaking like an umbilicus to the makeshift office. As buckets of newts came from the fields, each was caught and pressed against the glass while the beam of light scanned the belly. Understandably, it was the muckiest photocopier I've seen. Once copied, the newt went into another bucket which Rom and I happily ferried to the new site.

Another time, we went to Ipswich, East Anglia, to hunt snakes and lizards. It was a rare sunny weekend and we found non-venomous grass snakes, venomous adders and the legless slowworms (a lizard really). Soon we were stinking of snake poo; grass snakes are especially foul-smelling. Yet we couldn't stop as the sunshine was glorious and weather warm.

By far the strangest snake-hunting experience in the UK was in Bangor, Wales. In a fairly smallish park crawling with people doing various outdoorsy activities, were adders basking on tussocks of grass. The humans were blissfully ignorant of the little 'mines' underfoot. The weather was already cold and the animals were catching the last bit of sunshine before disappearing deep underground for the winter.

The rest of the time, when we weren't hunched over an editing table, we watched pigeons on Clifton Down, a large public park in Bristol. Occasionally a falcon would swoop down from a height and set the whole flock aflight. One day, a falcon caught a pigeon, and digging its talons into its struggling prey, began pulling feathers out to get to the jugular. An exuberant dog, happy to be out after a long day indoors, burst upon the scene. The startled falcon abandoned its prey and took off. The dog's owner came upon the half-dead pigeon and looked around guiltily. We averted our faces, pretending to be engrossed in a group of kids playing Frisbee, while surreptitiously watching the man. He wrung the pigeon's neck to put it out of its misery and threw it into the bushes before continuing on his way. Clifton Down was our sole hold on sanity.

We looked for every opportunity to be outdoors, as we were going stir crazy in our tiny apartment. We tried to do the city thing but jostling with people in pubs, theatres, homes, streets, and malls only made it worse. We were drugged flies struggling to find our way out of a large trap that was the city. You can take us out of the country but never the country out of us.

Naughty Words

We stumbled along a dark, narrow tunnel dug into a hill. Old pieces of timber held up the passageway but the walls were crumbling. One of the miners we had met in Puerto Jimenez, Costa Rica, the previous evening had mentioned seeing a tree boa regularly and there we were, that morning, looking for it. I muttered under my breath, 'This is a harebrained idea.'

Suddenly I heard Rom swear loud and clear. A disturbed tree boa had snapped the air in front of his face. The film crew following close behind had captured the entire action. No swearing is allowed on public television. Even bleeping out the swear word wasn't done because the audience can lip read. The crew wanted Rom to re-enact the scene. He couldn't imagine what else to say in a moment like that. On the second try, even as the snake made a half-hearted lunge, Rom exclaimed, 'Oops,' a mild word that fails to convey the initial shock. That's what happens when neither the presenter nor the snake are professional actors.

During the course of Rom's career as a presenter, this was a recurring problem. Many a good shot had to be sacrificed because of his inability to come up with an appropriate expression. Out of earshot of the crew I suggested, 'Swear in Tamil, Hindi or Pashto. The suits in Washington won't notice.' Rom has a vast vocabulary of expletives in several languages.

But even the resident multilingual cuss word expert didn't know that 'kumquat' was an offensive word. In 2011, the Pakistan Telecommunication Authority (PTA) issued a list of 1,109 offensive English words to be banned from text messages. 'Kumquat' was one of them. I thought it was simply a fruit tree. Mortified I may have committed a faux pas, I googled, checked English and American dictionaries, and there was no naughty connotation.

There were other equally puzzling words on what one Pakistani blogger calls the 'official expletive Thesaurus'. The word 'Budweiser' is banned but not 'Carlsberg', 'Foster's', 'alcohol', 'whisky' or any other kind of booze. The last is taboo if used in conjunction with a body part. One cannot describe Sachin Tendulkar as a 'master blaster' any more. Others include 'dome', 'harem', 'hostage', 'Kmart', 'robber', 'suicide' and many more. No doubt, many Pakistanis are flipping through dictionaries to discover what these seemingly innocent words *really* mean.

Three words are so foul that the PTA cannot bring itself to even mention them. In their stead are empty spaces and the Pakistanis have the unenviable job of figuring out what they may be. Like the blanks in Scrabble, the authorities could probably fill in anything they like depending on the context.

I suppose you never can tell who might find which words offensive. Some years ago I got into an argument with our neighbour. He wanted to chop down three old neem trees on our shared fence line. He claimed they cast a shadow on his crops, stunting their growth. That was a lie. He denuded the trees every year for green mulch. They hardly had a crown to cast a shadow. I suspected he wanted to sell them as firewood. I blurted, 'Nonsense!' He reacted so vehemently that I bit my tongue. Did I just curse, I wondered uncertainly. He shouted angrily, 'You called me "nonsense"?' Rom had to placate the man while I retreated hastily to the house. I don't use the word lightly anymore.

Rom, the cuss word expert, was unimpressed with PTA's list of 586 banned Urdu phrases. Apparently the choicest Pashto ones were missing. Maybe that's in the making, I suggested. As for me, at least here was a list with which to flummox our neighbour.

I realize young children may read this and learn a few naughty words. That wasn't my intention, kumquat!

Snakes in Drag

The earth seemed to be writhing and wriggling as more and more snakes emerged from crevices in the limestone. I was frozen to the spot; there seemed no space to take a step without squishing a few.

Red-sided garter snakes are small, slender snakes up to half a metre long, with a couple of parallel stripes running down their length. They are so named because they resemble the elastic bands that held stockings up in the old days. Individually, they are nondescript, but collectively they are a phenomenon. It was spring in Manitoba, Canada, and we were witnessing the emergence of the largest concentration of snakes anywhere in the world. By the end of the first day, I saw squirming snakes even when my eyes were closed.

I remember a scene in an old documentary of a woman briskly sweeping hundreds of garter snakes off her porch. Apparently, people living near the snake dens have to contend with this annual nuisance. We even heard of a couple who mistakenly built their home right atop a den and were overrun with these snakes. After a couple of years of this 'nightmare', the twosome relocated.

The May sun shone brightly but it did little to warm us

against the cold wind. I felt like doing little more than lazing in the sun. Yet, here were these cold-blooded animals busily courting and mating. For the last eight months, the snakes had brumated (similar to hibernation) deep underground, and I thought food would be their highest priority. No, being males, they had sex on their little minds. That may be because once they disperse across the countryside looking for frogs and snails, it's harder to find a mate. It's so much easier to hang around the dens and wait for the females to appear. Just like the scene outside some women's colleges.

Invariably, droves of males emerge first while the larger females come out in little groups. When she makes an appearance, several males jump on her, all at the same time, and within seconds she is buried under a mass of wriggling sex-starved maniacs. How's the poor, barely awake, harassed gal to choose a mate amongst the horde? Somehow, she does.

Adding a risqué note to this mating orgy were the transvestites. Males identify females by their scent. Intriguingly, some boy snakes give off an 'I am a girl, come-hither' perfume. What possible advantage could they gain by this subterfuge? Did they tire out the competition by sending them into a courtship frenzy and then mate with the females? Or were they just differently oriented?

Two scientists, Rick Shine and Robert Mason, figured that the transvestites did not gain any sexual mileage. When males emerge from the dens, they are cold and slow, but basking in the sun is like offering oneself on a platter to predators. By mimicking females, the cold males are immediately enveloped by warm, amorous males. Not only do the transvestites absorb heat from their suitors but by being buried under a pile of them, they are also well-protected from predators. Their first priority is not sex, but getting warm and being safe at the same time.

If transvestism is a survival advantage, doesn't it make sense for all males to act like females? They do. For the first two days after coming out of brumation, every male smells like a female. Once they warm up, they turn straight. Could this shared experience explain why the regular guys let themselves be fooled into protecting their rivals?

Do the transvestites become straight males halfway through the courtship, leaving a lot of confused suitors? After examining hundreds of snakes, the scientists found evidence of gay sex. How did they know? After copulation, the male inserts a gelatinous 'sperm' plug into the female's cloaca to prevent her from mating again. Some transvestites have been found with the tell-all plugs. I can well understand their excuse – it was too cold. And so was I.

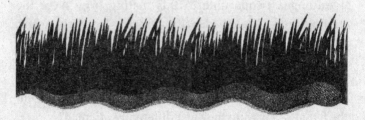

Ajoba's Story

His teeth were yellow, the canines were blunt; the leopard was in his prime. In late April 2009, while in hot pursuit of a dog, the cat fell into an open well in the agricultural farmlands of Takli Dokeshwar, north of Pune. Help arrived on the third night, when Forest Department staff lowered a ladder. The feline gingerly walked up and straight into a cage.

Vidya Athreya, a researcher, collared the leopard with a GPS transmitter before he was released 60 kms away at the foot of Malshej Ghats. For the next year, the collar would send text messages of the cat's whereabouts. That was how Ajoba became the first subject of a research project on farmland leopards.

Vidya expected him to make a beeline for the fertile farms and prowl amongst the fields of onions, cauliflower and sugarcane. Instead, he began climbing up the hills. That was odd.

Then Ajoba disappeared for three days. When the text messages resumed, he was on the other side of the ghats, down in the Konkan and across the busy Mumbai-Agra highway. 'What is he doing?' Vidya wondered in an e-mail.

Her heart was in her mouth when he crossed the Kasara railway station, the last stop for suburban trains from Mumbai. If he suffered even a minor mishap, it could be bad for the cat and the research project.

By the end of the third week, he had reached the Vasai Industrial Area, a vast spread of factories and buildings, on the outskirts of Mumbai. There was every chance that someone would spot the intruder and raise an alarm. Vidya was on tenterhooks. Older animals like Ajoba do not usually wander far from their established territories. So why was he walking purposefully westward?

The following week, Ajoba was in Nagla Block of the Sanjay Gandhi National Park, in Mumbai. When two weeks passed and he stayed in that one area, Vidya thought he had settled down. Ajoba had walked 120 kms in three and a half weeks. Then he swam across the Ullas river, entered the main park area for a three-day sojourn, and returned. Three weeks later, the GPS transmitter went dead. Perhaps the river crossings had shorted the circuitry.

It's possible that Sanjay Gandhi National Park was Ajoba's original home. In an effort to reduce leopard numbers in the park, he may have been moved to Malshej Ghats. But for the GPS tracker, we'd never have known about Ajoba's remarkable journey. He was close to people on several occasions, yet no one noticed him nor did he harm anybody.

Ajoba was a scientific pioneer, one who showed us that leopards are not jumpy, nervous animals, lashing out at humans at the slightest provocation. Despite the distance, speeding vehicles on highways, trains thundering along railways lines, and humans everywhere, he displayed a confident determination and an unerring sense of direction.

I never met Ajoba, but I felt drawn to the yellow dots tracing an arc on the map.

Soon after he was released, Vidya commented he had been calm, perhaps tired from his ordeal at the bottom of the well. During his travels, I imagined he kept his cool, always aware, alert, able to slip out of any sticky situation, and not prone to impulsive actions. I rooted for his survival, willed him to stay safe and cheered him on as he crossed yet another man-made barrier. And then we lost him.

Two and a half years later, on the night of 1 December 2011, a leopard was found dead, the victim of an accident, on the high-traffic Ghodbunder Road, about 12 kms from Nagla. Perhaps he misjudged the speed of the vehicle or been blinded by its headlights. Had there been an underpass to avoid crossing the treacherous road, he might still be alive. As is normal practice these days, the officials scanned him for a micro-chip. It read 00006CBD68F. Ajoba.

A Native Christmas

A few days ago, Rom and I were swapping stories about the most memorable Christmases of our lives. The one that stood out in my memory was when Madras was flooded after unusual rains in December. I was little and don't remember the year well. It was probably 1976. My parents and I were visiting friends, and I recall being shocked by the sight of their piano standing in stagnant water. I don't recall the goodies, the presents, or even how we travelled through the flooded city.

Rom said the most memorable Christmas he spent was in Irian Jaya, Indonesia, and I knew his story was going to be better than mine. In 1984, he was surveying crocs in the Rouffaer River, and Korodesi was the staging point. A couple of Christian missionary organizations operated the only conveyance service. There were no roads, cars, motorbikes, trains or any other means of surface transport in the interior. Villages along major rivers could be reached by boat; to go anywhere else, one needed to fly. Every major village had an airstrip for single engine planes.

When Rom woke up on Christmas morning, the entire village was already bustling with preparations for the *mumu* feast. Here's the recipe he readily shared.

IRIAN MUMU

Serves: 100
Preparation time: 6 hours

Ingredients:

100 kg meat (flying foxes, pythons, cassowaries, megapodes, wallabies, pigs, anything that moves), smoked and dried, or fresh and bloody, it doesn't matter.

100 kg vegetables (yams, tubers, squashes, pandanus fruit, raw green bananas, water weeds, greens)

Salt optional

Method:

Dig three huge pits in the ground, six feet deep and eight feet wide, and line them with banana leaves. Then start an enormous fire nearby. Haul about 200 boulders (about half to one kilo in weight each) from the nearest riverbank and throw them into the flames.

Once the rocks are molten hot, pile all the meat into the leaf-lined pits. Then layer with vegetables. Wrap the whole lot with more banana leaves. Ferry the hot river boulders one by one from the fire and stack them atop the leaves. The local way of doing this is to bring the ends of a length of green stick together and snap the hinge end. Grasp each boulder firmly between the two lengths, like using a nutcracker. Caution: the round rocks drop frequently. Ignore the many burns to feet, legs and hands.

Cover the pits with earth firmly. Cook for eight to nine hours. Bon appétit!

By evening the hot steaming mumu was opened and a feast followed. Rom dug into the sweet potatoes and the meat. There was even a Christmas cake – made of grubs. Large sago palm trees were chopped down for their pith, a staple in the local people's diet. Capricorn beetles laid eggs in the rotting stumps, and soon there were hundreds of plump, juicy white grubs, a much sought-after delicacy in these parts. Rom didn't care enough for the cake to write down the recipe.

As darkness fell, everyone was high, not on alcohol but from chewing betel nut. Some began singing and drumming while everyone else broke into dance. In a lull between songs, Rom found out they were singing Christian hymns set to their traditional music and in their own language. At his instigation, they switched to their old repertoire and danced boisterously.

The lead dancer was a cool dude called Maties. He had come to the party in his fancy costume – a bright yellow vest, long pants and red motorbike helmet with the vizor tilted back. The rest of his tribe was practically naked. In a land with no roads or motorbikes, the helmet had become a fashion accessory, one that cost Maties a croc skin. The singing and dancing continued all night long.

Our Christmas dinners are staid in comparison. Perhaps experimenting with the mumu for the next one might jazz it up.

The Nose Job

'The two male gharials are fighting and one has broken his nose,' the keeper said breathlessly. Rom and I ran to the enclosure. The other staff of the Madras Croc Bank also converged. It was the beginning of the breeding season and the younger male challenged the old reigning patriarch.

Their muscular tails churned the water, and their hot breaths – visible backlit against the early morning winter light – reminded me of illustrations of dragons of yore. It was a primeval, breathtaking spectacle. They turned their heads away from each other and brought them together with a bone-crunching slam. Their thin, long snouts are not made for this kind of battering. The old guy's upper jaw had snapped in half and dangled on one side. But they were still relentlessly going at each other.

The keepers stopped the fight by beating the water with long poles and yelling. Meanwhile, the broken jaw fell into the water. Rom ordered a search for it – easier said than done. All the gharial had to be chased out of the pond before the people could wade into the shallow water.

The staff formed a line at one end of the long water body and advanced slowly, feeling the bed with their bare feet.

Hours passed. It was early afternoon when one of the keepers dove underwater and surfaced triumphantly with the severed part. After blowing through the airway passage of the snout to clear debris and water, Rom positioned it against the raw wound on the gharial's jaw. With supporting splints, he strapped it up. One of the staff kept watch while the rest of us took a much-needed break.

At the dining table, I asked Rom, 'Don't you need to suture the croc up? How is the nose going to attach itself?' 'Crocs have remarkable healing powers,' he answered.

That is true. These reptiles get into some serious fights and suffer injuries, sometimes grievous ones. They seem to heal well, despite the unhygienic water conditions they live in. I can vouch for the filthiness of their aquatic habitat from personal experience. I had a minor cut on my foot while filming crocodiles in Sri Lanka. Within a couple of days of wading in the water, the wound had swollen up and I was running a temperature. It took a course of antibiotics to bring the infection under control.

About five years ago, Mark Merchant, a biochemist at McNeese State University in Louisiana, demonstrated what croc people had suspected for a long time. When a range of deadly pathogens, including HIV and West Nile virus, were introduced, antibodies in alligator blood destroyed them. Being a close relative, gharial probably had a similarly tough constitution. But could this croc reclaim a broken jaw?

The next morning, we stopped by the enclosure to check on the old warrior. He had spent the night rubbing and scratching, and had yanked the bandage off. The broken jaw lay nearby on the sand covered in flies. Croc blood may have powerful antibodies, but I didn't think it had little surgeons to reconnect severed nerves, arteries, and bone.

Eventually the reptile healed, but without his nose he could no longer snort like other adult male gharial. Nonetheless, the ladies appear to like him, and he is a prized stud of a critically endangered species.

The severed snout lies in a bath of formalin in the lab, a constant reminder of Rom's faith in the supernatural healing abilities of crocodilians. I sought the advice of croc vet, Paolo Martelli, who declared, 'There was no way in hell for the two fragments to reattach themselves.' Rom however, insists feebly, 'The wound was fresh. If the gharial hadn't yanked it off, it would have connected. Nerves migrate. Really.' His voice trailed.

Burmese Snakes and
Latino Plants

The abandoned railway station in Katerniaghat, near the border with Nepal, looked like a movie set of a bygone era. The dilapidated waiting rooms were filthy with the accumulated debris of several decades.

In one of the rooms, Rom picked up pieces of leathery, brown parchment from the floor. 'Python eggs,' he declared. He swung around and looked out through the doorway. I followed his gaze and thought, 'Uh oh.' Tall, raspy grass stretched down the gentle slope to a swamp overgrown with Ipomoea, a South American plant.

I plunged into the grass after Rom; it was almost my height. If I didn't keep up with him, the vegetation swung back like a curtain and covered his tracks. The blades of grass sliced my hands as I held them out to protect my face. I was probably small enough to be python food, I thought with discomfort. But it was too late to retreat now.

When we emerged onto the swamp, Rom began looking around. He held up his hand signalling me to stop. Something plopped into the water not far from us.

The spindly, rangy Ipomoea grew in a tangled mass and cradled the basking pythons well above the water. As an added bonus, when predators or snake-hunters like Rom arrived, the vibrations passed along the lattice work of plant stalks for several yards, like telegraph, alerting the sunbathing snakes. Long before we got close, we heard the crackling of dry twigs followed by the sound of a snake slipping into the water.

We stood still, wondering how to find a python, when one found us. A large snake approached Rom, flicking its tongue at his heels curiously. Its eyes were cataract opaque; it would go into skin-shedding mode in a few days. Usually snakes in this vulnerable stage of blindness hunker quietly in a dark hollow.

Without wasting a minute, Rom picked it up. He wanted to check if this was an Indian or a Burmese rock python. They are both the same species but with a few differences. Rom ordered, 'Check the suboculars.' I looked at the ring of scales around the eye in bewilderment. Rom was having a hard time controlling a squirming 12-foot snake, so I was on my own. I looked for other distinguishing characteristics.

The python had a clear arrowhead marking on the top of its head, the tongue was blue-black and the face had no hint of pink. All signs of a Burmese rock python. When Rom released it, it shot through the thicket with a speed that belied its bulk. I felt certain that snake would never make the mistake of approaching a human again.

We stood little chance of finding any more pythons in the swamp. That evening, we returned to investigate the abandoned railway station. In one room, we not only found pieces of eggshell but also numerous tracks of baby snakes etched faintly in the dust. For more than a century, pythons were slaughtered countrywide for their skin and now, three decades after the ban, they were obviously doing well in some places at least.

Burmese pythons are also flourishing on the other side of the planet, in the Everglades of Florida. They have gained a notorious reputation as predators of local mammals, alligators and birds. The seed population was probably released by irresponsible pet owners. Snake-hunters and wildlife officials kill every python they see but it's debatable if they'll ever be rid of them.

In Katerniaghat, however, the snakes rely on a foreign species for their protection. To a purist, Ipomoea may be an eyesore that ought to be removed from a protected sanctuary. No doubt, it supplants local species which would have benefitted a greater number of creatures. However, until a native replacement is found, the Latino alien provides refuge to this population of Burmese pythons.

Plant's Poison, Man's Potion

For years, I've been feeding used coffee grounds and tea leaves to a couple of bird's-nest ferns in our garden. It was better than clogging the drain or mucking up the garbage can. Besides, it is good organic mulch for plants that need plenty of it. Visitors often remark about the bright green, three-foot-long, luxuriant fronds.

In my imagination, the plants are nervous wrecks, insomniacs on a caffeine overdose. Unable to rest, perhaps they don't have a choice but to keep growing. I then began to wonder why coffee plants produce caffeine. Why do they need it?

Plants, like other living beings, don't want to be eaten. Even if they can't run away from their predators, they are far from helpless. Some acacias draft ants to fight their battles. They secrete sweet-tasting sap to encourage the insects to take up residence in their branches. Should a herbivore attack the tree, the bite-happy creatures mount a formidable defence and chase the animal away.

Some plants grow thorns and spines that deter browsing animals. Nettles, for instance, are covered in sharp minute hairs loaded with histamine. Any hungry herbivore has to merely brush against the plant to learn a lasting lesson.

Some plants have become sophisticated chemistry labs, synthesizing bitter compounds to make their leaves and seeds distasteful, even poisonous. This is a battle of adaptation, spanning millennia and thousands of species.

Some animals have the upper hand, able to digest a toxic salad of their favourite plants. In the ninth century, Ethiopian shepherds noticed their flocks acting unusually frisky after eating wild red berries in the highlands. Those plants were domesticated and coffee is now cultivated in 80 countries. Today, it is said to be the most traded commodity after crude oil. Every year, 400 billion cups of the beverage are drunk by people seeking a caffeine fix. Others prefer caffeinated tea or soft drinks for the same reason – to attain a heightened state of alertness. Ironically, the cup we drink to refresh ourselves when our energies flag is an alkaloid produced by plants to put to sleep insects that have designs on their seeds. In other words, we are addicted to an insecticide that evolved to paralyze and kill.

Caffeine affects even insect predators dramatically. In the late 1990s, scientists at NASA illustrated the effects of various drugs on the web-spinning abilities of spiders. The eight-legged creature fared disastrously under the influence of caffeine. It strung a few threads in a chaotic, random pattern that bore little resemblance to a web it would have spun under normal circumstances. Generally, insects leave the plant alone, except coffee borer beetles which have developed immunity.

A lot of humans are addicted to caffeine but many more are addicted to tobacco. The nicotine found in the leaves is another powerful neurotoxic insecticide. Besides protecting themselves, the plants have another use for the drug. Their nectar is tainted with it, but they are not trying to poison their pollinators; that would be self-destructive. The plants want them to be brief and move on, and the nicotine discourages insects from drinking long and deep. So the pollinators have to visit more plants to get a full meal. In doing so, they traffic pollen among many plants increasing their genetic diversity. And the insects are apparently hooked to the nicotine. In experiments, they demonstrated their preference for caffeine or nicotine-tainted nectar to the plain, safe kind. But they like just enough for a buzz, not too much to paralyze them, not too little to be uninteresting.

Besides feeding our vices, we have enlisted the aid of plants in our own war against pathogens. Quinine in Cinchona was the frontline anti-malarial drug for more than two centuries. With increasing drug-resistance in many parts of the world, artemisin, a compound isolated from a Chinese plant, is the current life-saver.

We don't only use plant compounds to treat dreaded diseases – our headache pills (aspirin) come from willows, while morphine and a range of painkillers are derived from opium. The seeds of the beautiful glory-lily, Tamil Nadu's state flower, are used to treat gout and may have anti-cancer properties. In fact, any new medical challenge sends humans scouring the plant world for a cure.

Besides, plants are known pest-repellents. Rom's mom inter-planted marigolds with tomatoes to keep the latter free of bugs. Neem is another widely used pesticide.

But I was surprised to find two-inch-long, slender, green, hairless caterpillars of a moth voraciously strip every bitter-tasting leaf from neem saplings. Entomologist, Gunathilagaraj Kandasamy, says caterpillars of three moths and a butterfly species are known pests of neem, the natural pesticide.

Caterpillars are slow-moving and easy pickings for predators. Like the plants on which they survive, several sprout a formidable array of irritating hairs and sharp spines. The most lethal of them all are the hairy Lonomias from South America which are known to kill humans. A few naked caterpillars accumulate plant alkaloids in their own soft bodies, becoming a dangerous meal for any bird looking for an easy worm. By extension, these plants are anti-predator weapons.

By feeding our needs, whether it be addictive drugs, spices or cures for diseases, plants have unwittingly ensured their widespread propagation by humans. But that's not all. They even help us get in touch with the spiritual which, according to some philosophers, is the defining characteristic of being human.

In the deserts of the New World, cacti may be one of the few sources of hydration for animals. Most plants have sharp thorns or spines to protect their succulent bodies. But the peyote cactus appears to have traded prickliness for a powerful psychedelic alkaloid, mescaline. There is no known peyote predator except man in search of visions. Some suspect soma, the Indian elixir of immortality, 'creator of the Gods', to be a plant, although its identity remains shrouded in mystery.

As for my ferns, I learnt it may be the potassium and phosphorus in the coffee grounds that makes them luxuriant. Too much caffeine may be bad and my ferns are likely to  grow with renewed vigour if I hold back the drug. Well, at least they won't go into caffeine withdrawal. Or will they?

Bringing up Luppy

When I was five, I saw a sounder of feral pigs mucking about in Thanjavur. I may have seen others before, but in my memory, that was the first. I was instantly captivated by the piglets and gushed, 'They are so cute.' My uncle commented all animals are cute as babies and pointed to the scruffy, filth-coated sow. Undeterred, I fantasized about living on a farm with pigs when I grew up.

Decades later, Rom and I visited our friend, Rohan Mathias, in Masinagudi. Walking around his property, we came upon a large open-air enclosure that held four huge Yorkshire sows and piglets of various sizes. Two of the piglets were brown with white stripes and had prominent manes, like the wild species that roamed the neighbouring forests. Apparently, an agile wild boar had jumped over the low masonry wall, mated with a sow and escaped. Rohan generously gifted us one of the striped piglets.

We drove back home with mutinous squeals ringing in our ears. Finally, my dream of getting a pet pig was being realized. Since I had no clue how to raise a piglet, Luppy grew up with the dogs. She was smart and learnt to sit, lie down, jump, and roll over on command.

When she was half-grown, she turned into a pest. The first casualty was a passion fruit vine; she chewed through the stem and killed it. Then assorted house plants I had collected from far and wide were chomped, pulled up by the roots and dropped somewhere in the garden. She wasn't trying to eat them; she was only tasting, but that was enough to kill the plant. She just tossed her head in defiance when I reprimanded her.

Full-grown, she was built like a tank and strong as a baby rhino. When she was well-fed, she was obedient and tractable. With her gargantuan appetite, the well-behaved periods were short-lived. Most of the time, she ran riot, scattering geese and hens, eating bamboo shoots, killing saplings, and often barging into the kitchen taking anything edible within reach. Once she grabbed a tidbit, it was hers. It disappeared into her maw in an instant. At feeding time, she usurped one of the dogs' bowls and they resented the competition. As a solution, we built an enclosure for her.

Summer arrived and we feared Luppy would be tempted by our neighbours' newly flooded fields in preparation for planting rice. She was strong enough to break through the barbed wire fence, if she set her mind to it. At home, she could be lured into her enclosure with a head of cabbage. But if she got loose in the neighbours' farms, I wasn't confident she'd obey. She had a mind of her own and there is nothing a pig loves more than to wallow on a hot summer day. So we created a muddy puddle in her enclosure.

We worried she might be lonely and asked a local pig owner if we could get a boar. I wanted a full-grown male who was as tame as Luppy. The man nodded his head hesitantly. Rom later said that the man's pigs ran feral through the town eating garbage, like those ones I had seen decades ago, and there was no chance he would have a docile one.

A few days later, the man arrived with a boar, a third the size of Luppy. I suggested keeping them separate until they got to know each other. The man overruled me and introduced the little boar to Luppy. After an initial exploratory sniff, she attacked. She tossed him in the air and he squealed loudly and piteously. We rescued the fellow before she did any further harm.

Today, 11-year-old Luppy lives in solitary contentment, watching the goings-on in the farm, grunting at newcomers and presenting her belly for a scratch. And my reputation in the family as that-girl-who-loves-dirty-pigs is sealed.

The 'Blarry' Rascals

Rom was awakened by the sound of a car scrunching over gravel at 2 a.m. He looked out the window and saw his car sliding downhill. Swearing under his breath for not putting the hand brake on, he braced himself for the inevitable crash when the car collided with the gate. But surprisingly, the brake lights went on. Suddenly Rom was sleepy no more. Thieves! Barefoot and still in his *lungi*, he ran outside, yelling and screaming. Instead of escaping with the vehicle, the car thieves ran away

The gate was locked and they hadn't been able to jimmy it open, so the burglars had unravelled the chain link fence. They could have driven off with the car, except a large eucalyptus tree blocked the path. Had they made an opening anywhere else on the fence, they could have made a clean getaway. Even then, in the early 1980s, Rom felt the 'rascal problem', as it was called euphemistically ('blarry lascots' in slang Pidgin, which in English means 'bloody rascals'), was out of hand in Port Moresby, the capital of Papua New Guinea (PNG), where he spent two years on a crocodile project.

That wasn't Rom's only run-in with rascals. One night, he

returned home late after a movie to find someone had forced the door open. Careful not to make a noise, he tiptoed into the house. It was empty but he found a screwdriver lying on the floor. A torch lay nearby, its batteries spilled out. Something had frightened the thieves away.

It was probably a pair of green tree pythons that lived in the large window near the door. Every window had glass louvre panes on the inside and a mosquito screen on the outside. Rom added a couple of branches and the enclosed windowsill had ample space to hold snakes. Being the snake nut that he was, every window doubled as a terrarium. While looking for valuables to steal, the burglars must have seen the snakes and scrammed.

When Rom travelled to the interior on field trips, he hired a tribal warrior to guard the house. Around that time, PNG was going through a transition. A lot of the Australian and New Zealand expat workers were leaving and their posts were being filled by Asians. The Filipinos confronted the rascal problem head-on. One of them showed Rom a wooden replica of a pistol he had fashioned, complete with a barrel hole. Each end of a strip of very high tensile rubber was attached to either side of the 'pistol'. The 'bullets' were six-inch iron nails whose heads had been sawn off, and the business end sharpened and tapered. The 'pistol' is held with the left hand, and like a catapult, the rubber is pulled back while gripping the nail. It was accurate and deadly.

The situation in PNG is even worse now. Last year, when a friend was away from home, five men smashed into his house at 3 a.m., ripping the four steel security doors from their hinges. They punched his wife, and pointing a gun to her head demanded car keys, money, credit cards, and other valuables. Once they decamped, the lady and her son ran next door for help.

After this incident, our friend installed four extra heavy-duty security doors, surveillance cameras around the house, an alarm system, emergency radios monitored by an armed response company, hired two full-time security guards, bought an attack dog, and even stocked some firearms. It may seem like overkill, but while the rascals were mainly looking for food and booze in the old days, they have become hardened criminals. Besides, even some law enforcement officers were not beyond suspicion.

I told our friend, 'Had I been in your place, I would have gotten the hell out of there, pronto.' I doubt I have the strength of character his wife showed, all the modern weapons and security systems notwithstanding. He replied, 'I didn't marry a delicate princess.'

The Making of Croc Bank

We walk down the main path of the Madras Crocodile Bank as we've done countless times before. But this time I ask Rom to narrate how the place took shape. 'The process took 10 years at least,' Rom says.

In the early 1970s, crocs had a hard time worldwide. Rom did the first croc surveys in India and found the three Indian species struggling to survive. It was the usual gripe of habitat loss and poaching. Tony Pooley in Zimbabwe and Ted Joanen in the States were breeding Nile crocs and alligators respectively and restocking wild populations. Rom felt he could do the same for the mugger, the gharial, and saltwater crocs in India. That was why the Croc Bank was set up.

Rom and his then-wife, Zai, invested their wedding gift of Rs 14,000 in the new venture. Rom went farther and farther down the road to Mahabalipuram until he found land within his budget. Since it was sandy, he would just need to scoop out a hole to hit the water table and create a pool. Tourism was still a nascent industry but Rom could see the potential. This was crucial as a long-term strategy, since in later years, the gate collection was to fund many conservation projects in the wild.

Land was available in strips, just 10 to 20 feet wide, but about 1,000 feet long. 20 different negotiations later, Rom had a 10-acre spread from the road to the beach. Each deal was sealed by the seller and purchaser downing a litre of fermented palm toddy. Rom remembers staggering home by early afternoon.

We come to the large enclosure with thick granite walls, now called Enclosure Eight. It housed the first stock of 14 mugger crocs. Within a year, these animals produced close to a 100 offspring. Rom didn't know then that crocs were scaly rabbits.

In those days, only a few spindly casuarina trees grew on the land. Ignoring the accepted wisdom that only coconut trees and casuarinas would grow on the sandy beach, Rom sourced hundreds of broad-leaved native species like Pongamia and Albizzia from forest department nurseries and Auroville. The staff's only accommodation was thatched huts.

Croc Bank was opened to the public in 1976, the first tourist facility on, what was later to become, the East Coast Road. Jimmy Yacob, a landscape architect from Johor, Malaysia, planned the central pathway with enclosures flanking the sides. Since the land sloped from the road to the beach, he levelled it into terraces.

Although Rom liked the solid walls of Enclosure Eight, money was short and more enclosures were needed for the gharial, saltwater crocs, and the baby croc nurseries. Brick walls were cheaper. But he didn't have money to make them the regular nine inches thick, so he made single-brick walls supported by concrete pillars every five to six feet.

We reach the end where the gharial enclosure is located.

Since it is a riverine species, Rom says he created a pool that resembles a river bend. The excavated sand forms the Gharial Mound behind the enclosure. In the early 1990s, when I began living there, the hillock was a quiet place to laze under the trees and read a book. If it was dull, I would roll over and watch tourists. On some warm afternoons, I'd fall asleep to the mournful creaking of the windmill nearby.

The windmill was meant to pump up water from the gharial enclosure to feed a waterfall at one end of the pool. But the windmill was badly designed and needed more headwind than blew off the sea. The waterfall remained a dream and the windmill was consigned to the scrap heap.

Over the past 35 years, the trees have grown, while the collection has more than 2,000 crocs of 18 species, and 19 species of snakes, lizards and turtles. The Croc Bank is India's largest reptile park.

A Moveable Feast

Before I met Rom, everyone I knew thought termites were pests. When the rains first arrive, clouds of these winged creatures swarm. They buzz around lights and eventually drown in our beverages and dinners. The rest of the year, diligent workers find devious ways of attacking wood furniture. Friends who cry, 'Herbal mozzie repellent only please', nuke termites with awful chemicals without a second thought.

When Rom and I moved to our farm, I realized a termite swarm is a major natural history event. Termites are a rich source of protein that every creature regards as a feast. As the insects soared on their conjugal flights, watchful drongos made acrobatic sorties snapping them up.

Once termites find mates, they lose their wings and burrow underground to nest. Lacking superior aerial skills, shikras perched ungainly on the ground, pecking at these wingless ones. The birds' prime prey – garden lizards – also engorged themselves. They scurried noisily through the dry leaf litter aware that for the moment, their nemesis preferred the fat succulent bodies of these insects to their own scaly, tough ones. Nearby, a flock of white-capped babblers competed with magpie-robins and bulbuls in chasing termites through the grass.

Toads sat like statues, only their tongues flicking in and out mechanically. These were especially greedy little buggers, stuffing themselves more and more when they couldn't even waddle out of the way. Scorpions rammed so many insects down their throats that the wings stuck out of their mouths, making them look like feathered chimeras.

Perhaps this was the only occasion when nocturnal and diurnal creatures, predators and prey dined together. We once found a monitor lizard lying draped over a termite mound, sated, incapable of movement. Even palm squirrels, which I thought were vegetarians, joined in. The normally alert mongooses were so focused on stuffing themselves that they didn't notice our presence.

Our two young emus were nowhere near as proficient as the others in finding termites. With their large round eyes affixed on an insect in flight, they chased it round and round in comical circles, only occasionally snatching one from midair. Later when the sun rose higher in the sky and the swarming died out, life returned to normal.

The arrival of the rains is the cue for the insects to take off on their nuptial flights. But the Irula tribals are wizards in exploiting this resource even without a shower. Many years ago, on a moonless night, I watched them tie a sari around a mound to simulate the stillness before rain. A tin can was buried in the ground. An oil lamp, the only source of light, was balanced on cross-sticks on top of the can. They blew the powder of a local seed called *eessal kottai* (termite nut), which smelt of rain, over the mound. They chanted with a lot of sibilance, like the whispering wings of termites.

Initially nothing happened and I thought this was all hocus-pocus. Then the termites started emerging. They were unable to fly; perhaps their wings were not fully formed yet. They headed for the light and fell into the can. Soon, hundreds of thousands of them came pouring out like a black river. The Irula emptied the can into a gunny sack every few minutes and within an hour, the sack was half full.

Back at the Irula hamlet, we gathered around the fire as they roasted the insects on an iron griddle with rice, turmeric and chilli powder and salt. The fat from the termites sizzled and made the rice grains pop. When I gingerly sampled a roasted termite, I could barely taste it. I followed the Irula example and shoved a whole handful into my mouth. And then another. Was it insects I was eating? They tasted of fried nuts with a buttery texture but the flavour was unique. Like those toads, I couldn't stop stuffing myself. With a knowing grin, one of the Irula asked me how the midnight snack tasted.

I answered in Tamil, 'Super.'

The Price of Gold

The main street of Puerto Jiménez, Costa Rica, was packed with shops stocked with everything from large televisions, refrigerators, washing machines to toasters and food processors. There seemed to be more appliances than the town's population. Whom were these shops trying to entice?

We were making a film about snakes of Costa Rica, and Johnny, a native Costa Rican (or 'tico'), was our translator. Since gold miners in this area frequently encountered snakes, we relied on a couple of them as our guides.

As we followed the miners into the forest, I bombarded them with questions. Did they find a lot of gold? When was the last time they found some? One of our miner-guides had unearthed a nugget of gold the previous week. Later, I held the chunk of metal; it was the size of my fist and looked like an abstract sculpture. I noticed that another chap wore an attractive gold pendant on a shoelace around his neck. It was gorgeous and unique. Where could I find more like it, I asked, thinking it was locally crafted.

Not so easy, Johnny replied. It was of local origin all right, but from another time and civilization. The pendant was thousands of years old and came from an ancient tomb.

The wearer was a part-time tomb-raider. The movie *Lara Croft: Tomb Raider* had just been released and this guy didn't look anything like Angelina Jolie.

'Do you want to see more ancient jewellery?' the miner asked. Later at his house, he displayed clay and stone figurines of jaguars and other animals he had unearthed with the beautiful ornaments. These treasures belonged in a museum and to find them in someone's house was astonishing.

Despite the high prices gold fetched, the miners were mostly broke, living on credit. When they found a nugget of gold, like most jackpot winners, they went on a shopping spree, stocking their houses with every appliance. There were enough miners and there was enough gold for the shops to remain open six days a week. As we drove by, I peered inside looking for anyone trading chunks of metal. The shops were disappointingly empty.

Although the adrenalin rush of finding sudden riches is heady, gold mining is fraught with risks. These men dug deep into forested hillsides looking for the yellow metal. The tunnels were held up by rickety beams of timber and the risk of collapse was high. Some were buried alive before they could be excavated while many others escaped with injuries. After hearing these stories, when we entered the narrow tunnels in search of tree boas, I suffered from severe claustrophobia. Rom, however, bravely entered where sensible women feared to tread.

During their daily toil, miners and tomb-raiders also had to brave dangerous snakes, like fer-de-lance. Locally called 'terciopelo' ('velvet' in Spanish), these are gorgeous, lethal snakes that are completely camouflaged in forest leaf litter.

Even when Rom pointed one out, I just could not see the snake until I got closer. I tried to train my eyes to be sharper. I looked elsewhere at the forest trees and glanced back at the snake. I could have sworn it had disappeared until Rom painstakingly described its location again.

We interviewed a former miner who had a nasty encounter with a terciopelo. A long scar ran from his elbow to the back of his mangled hand. He narrated how doctors had to slice the ballooning arm to relieve pressure. A couple of his fingers were inflexible and the one that took the bite was missing a chunk. He described the intolerable pain he suffered and the many months of recovery. He didn't mine for gold anymore, he said.

Like the terciopelo, those flashy shops in Puerto Jiménez camouflaged the price paid by these miners, in broken limbs, lost livelihoods, and lives. They also hid the massive scar snaking across the region's environment and cultural history caused by mining and tomb-raiding.

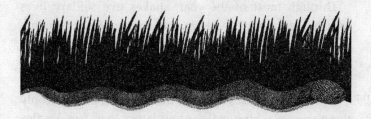

Snake Wrestlers

Snakes do not dance. Humans do, birds do. But snakes don't. What most people call the 'mating dance' is actually a wrestling match between two male snakes of the same species.

In towns and villages across Southern India, carved stone sculptures of snakes intertwined in combat are installed under trees near temples. These fertility offerings are made by couples who want to conceive a son.

Through most of the year, snakes live solitary lives focusing on hunting, basking, and resting. When breeding season comes, some active species travel far and wide looking for mates and territorial boundaries blur. Combat then becomes necessary to establish the boss.

Not all male snakes show off their fighting prowess; only those species whose males grow larger than females flex their muscles. But there are exceptions. Male cobras, for instance, are larger than females, but don't wrestle. In species with larger females, she chooses her mate from the bevy of suitors writhing all over her.

Among the fighting species, male snakes have no illusions about their machismo. Instead of stupidly challenging large dudes, small guys slink away into the bushes and wait to fight another day. When two virile snakes are evenly matched and both think they are better endowed, a duel ensues.

How does a tubular animal with no arms or legs wrestle? They could bite each other, but that would leave them both with severe injuries. It would be worse if they had venom. These supremely civilized creatures have evolved a code of honour; they keep their mouths firmly shut through the entire bout. Survival plays umpire.

Duelling snakes twine their lower bodies around each other, rise high up off the ground and try to slam the opponent to the ground. Their heads weave higher and higher in midair as each tries to gain the height necessary to throw the rival down. Their fluid and graceful movements seems more like dance than battle. It can go on for an hour and saps the snakes of energy. Stamina is a prime criterion for winning. The one who tires and gives up first is the loser.

After recuperating, a defeated snake could challenge the victor again. There is probably much at stake if he's willing to invest so much energy in dislodging one dominant male. As with many male-male competitions, women are probably the cause. There's often a female snake in the vicinity of such coiled combat.

When two snakes are engrossed in each other, they become oblivious to their surroundings. A pair of large king cobras fought a long, hard battle across a bridge in Karnataka while people parked their vehicles and gathered around to watch. Unmindful of spectators, snakes have fought in rice fields, courtyards of farmhouses, and plantations.

Once, while watching a pair of king cobras jousting, one of them suddenly slithered off at great speed. Rom was right in his way, and caught on the wrong foot, couldn't move fast enough. He did the next best thing – stood stock still. The 11-foot-long snake shot between his legs, and a split second later, reached up and bit Rom on the bum. Rom knew something terrible was happening just from seeing my horrified expression. In the tense silence of the moment, the sound of the king cobra's numerous teeth ripping through denim rent every cord of my heart. A second later, the snake was gone.

We crowded around Rom, examining his rear end for drops of blood. Fortunately, the fangs hadn't made contact with skin. While we were still shaken, Rom joked that had he been bitten, he would have found out who his friends were. Seeing my blank expression, he said with a wink, 'Only a true friend would suck the venom out.'

Scent of a Dog

Dear Ma,

Ever since you forcibly gave us all a bath on Sunday, we've been meaning to explain our side of the story. It is true, Momo rolled on jackal poo. You accused her of smelling 'rank', but we disagree. To us, she smelt heavenly. If we had a chance, we'd have made a beeline for the spot and rolled in it too. We can't explain why we do it.

You human animals have various theories. One says we do it to disguise our telltale doggie smell to creep up on unsuspecting little birds and squirrels. But why would we mask our scent with another predator's? Besides, are we idiots to exchange our slight doggie smell for a strong one that is noticeable miles away? Sometimes you humans are dumb.

Biologists think wolves, our distant cousins, roll in carrion so pack members know there's food to be had and what it smells like. But they also roll in excreta. Although we don't get along with wolves, we'll grudgingly acknowledge they are not depraved enough to eat their own or anyone else's faeces. They will if they are starving but not otherwise. So why then roll on poo?

Let's just say, we are hopelessly attracted to smelly stuff, whether it is jackal faeces or a long dead bird or rat. Those wolves are only telling their pack like Momo told us, 'Hey guys, there's some really heady stuff over there to roll on. Here, sniff.' You like the bright colours of flowers, clothes and paintings, and we like loud smells. We might roll on flowers if only they smelt stronger.

We pee and poo around the garden to mark our territory. Other dogs sniffing our scent-bombs will be able to tell that we are three girls and one boy, that Koko is old and Bhima is young, and that we'd beat them up if they set foot on our domain. Had you not fixed the girls, boy dogs could tell when they come on heat.

One thing is for sure though, we hate the smell of shampoo and we struggle to get rid of it. But you prohibit us from even rolling on warmed-by-the-sun green grass. That is our biggest complaint.

Smell is important to you humans too, except you won't accept it. We don't know how to say this gently but that new stink bottle you bought the other day? Well, it's disgusting. We smirked when you read the label out loud to Pa, 'A floral fragrance with top notes of bergamot, neroli, and jasmine. With this *eau de parfum* you will experience the sensual essence that makes you feel special.' We think it makes you smell less human and more like a creature from outer space cloaked in artificial chemicals.

You know when you smell the best? When you play with us in the evenings. You get hot and sweaty and all your scent pores open up wide. That is the true you, the real you. Have you not noticed how Pa reacts to that mongoose-y scent? No, you haven't. You may be embarrassed to hear this but your scent reveals your hormonal levels, your emotional status and receptivity to him. Then you ruin it by showering and smearing all kinds of smelly goo. Sheesh!

If it helps to understand us better, think of jackal poo as our eau de parfum, that we like to wear to make ourselves sensually special. We realize Momo sleeps under your table and a strong smell would distract you. So can we reach a compromise please? We will willingly go for a bath if we smell unacceptable to your genteel senses. But could we roll on grass after that please? That's all we ask.

Love you,

Koko, Lola, Momo and Bhima (in hierarchical order)

PS: One more thing, please throw away that stink bottle and join us on the grass.

A Tale of Two Sambhars

You could say it began with the word 'sambhar'. What does sambhar, the South Indian dish, have in common with sambhar, the Asian deer? Was the animal named for the stew or vice versa? In all four Southern states where the dish is made, it is called sambhar. However, the animal is called sambhar in Hindi. Is this a case of the parallel evolution of the word in different languages? The dual meaning and almost identical pronunciation of the word led to some exasperating bilingual conversations in forest camps.

My curiosity about the origins of words began when I began to probe the provenance of trees. About 20 years ago, an ecologist mentioned that neem may not be Indian. He had heard it from someone else and couldn't name a definite source. Astonished, I asked botanists and tree planters, and read different sources in an effort to find the tree's true homeland.

Botanical authorities, Dietrich Brandis and Marius Jacobs, said the dry forests of Upper Irrawaddy, Burma, may be neem's home. James Sykes Gamble speculated it was the forests of Karnataka, or the dry inland forests of Burma.

J.F. Duthie and U.N. Kanjilal thought it originated in the Shiwaliks, Uttarakhand. The east coast of India and even Africa were mentioned by others.

But Heinrich Schmutterer argued that neem displays a wide range of differences in physical features in Burma, which suggests greater genetic diversity. Therefore, that country is likely to be its motherland. Many, however, vehemently disagree and insist it is native to India. Perhaps a molecular study will reveal the original home of this tree.

Today, neem is found in tropical dry deciduous, tropical dry evergreen, and thorn forests. On our farm, a whole variety of fruit-eating birds like golden orioles, cuckoos, and bulbuls feast on the fruits and disperse seeds. Neem is the food plant of a few species of moths. Whether it originated in Karnataka, Uttarakhand or Burma, the species has colonized the rest of the country with considerable help from man.

What about other quintessentially Indian trees? Despite its widespread use, tamarind doesn't belong here either.

So how did sambhar come to be?

Sambhaji, Shivaji's son, was a guest at the court of his cousin, Shahuji I, a Maratha king who ruled Thanjavur, Tamil Nadu, in the 18th century. When the host was making *amti*, he ran out of kokum from his homeland, and he substituted tamarind. And that's how sambhar was born and the new dish was named in honour of the guest, Sambhaji. The Maratha origin of sambhar is a known oral story. If sambhar is a derivative of Sambhaji's name – which in turn harks back to Sambha, son of Krishna, or Sambhu, an epithet of Siva – what's the connection to the deer?

The root of the animal's name is the Sanskrit '*œambara*'. In

Hindu mythology, Indra slew a demon of that name. Was the animal named after a villain? Or is it, like the stew, named for Sambhu, 'lord of the universe', who is depicted holding a deer in one of his hands? I can only speculate.

As Rom ladles another scoop of sambhar into a cup, he asks mischievously, 'All the history and name play is nice, but how about a sambhar sambhar?'

21st Century Idli

During winter months, my mother goes through a lot of trouble keeping *idli* batter warm enough through the night. She even wraps an old woollen sweater around the container. During fermentation, as many as 276 species of bacteria belch carbon dioxide and ooze lactic acid into the batter. Like all women who are proud of the soft, light fluffiness of their idli, my mother makes life comfortable for the microbes.

For being so quintessentially South Indian, the process of making idli may not be indigenous at all. Food scientist, K.T. Achaya, in *A Historical Dictionary of Indian Food*, quoted the famous 7th century Chinese traveller, Xuan Zang categorically stating that India did not have a steaming vessel, critical to idli preparation as we know it today. Achaya also suggested that Indonesians make a dumpling, similar to the idli, called *kedli*. But there is little evidence a dish of that name exists. It was only between the 8th and 12th centuries that we South Indians borrowed fermenting and steaming techniques from Indonesia.

Idli is a vehicle for sambhar to go down. And my compadres are renowned to put it away by the gallon. The disappointing news, of course, is sambhar is not South Indian either.

Marathi amti is flavoured by *kokum*, a concentrate made from the fruit of a forest tree in the Western Ghats. When kokum was replaced with tamarind, which was brought to India thousands of years ago from Africa, amti became sambhar. (Even though the name, *tamar-ul-hind*, means 'date of India' in Arabic, its African ancestry is not disputed.) South Indians uniquely coupled a dumpling whose texture is Indonesian with an Afro-Marathi stew and made it their own.

We wash that delectable breakfast down with cups of coffee. Coffee may be from Ethiopia but South Indians brew a sweet and mean filter *kapi*. In my family, the 'tradition' of drinking this beverage began with my parents' generation. My grandparents and great-grandparents drank coffee only on special occasions. One great-grandmother drank a non-caffeinated beverage made of roasted coriander seeds and dried ginger called 'coriander coffee'. She may not have known that coriander was domesticated in the Mediterranean and ginger probably in Southeast Asia.

Cooking techniques and foreign ingredients fertilized Europe too. According to one story, Marco Polo introduced Chinese noodles, which later became spaghetti, to his homeland in the 13th century. While another suggests that noodles may have followed ancient trade routes preceding the intrepid traveller by centuries. However, many believe pasta is a home-grown invention. Whatever be pasta's past, tomatoes in the sauce are without a doubt American. Like South Indians, Italians borrowed elements from elsewhere to come up with spaghetti smothered in tomato sauce.

Many of the vegetables we use everyday – cabbage, potato, pumpkin, carrot, and beans – are not Indian. What did we eat before this cornucopia arrived on our shores? Perhaps some gourds, leafy vegetables, some legumes, a range of yams, parts of banana trees like pith, flowers, and green fruit. None of which Rom will touch, not even with a fork at the end of a barge pole. However, any mention of the wild game ancient South Indians may have eaten is enough to make his carnivorous palate salivate.

Two decades ago, friends and cousins of my generation left for the US with heavy pressure cookers in their suitcases. Now, for grinding idli batter, nephews and nieces pack heavier 'wet grinders' which even come in 110 volt versions. Not content serving us idli in their homes, when we visit them in California, they proudly take us to the nearest Udupi restaurant. It's as if we never left home.

The origin of plant species interests me greatly. If Africans tamarind-flavoured many a dish long before sambhar, I wondered what our cuisine was like before being influenced by foreign elements. Instead of finding recipes with native plants, I discovered that, unlike us, our forefathers and mothers were global citizens borrowing cooking techniques and experimenting with imported ingredients.

We, their conservative descendants, however, have eaten the idli in the same form for nine centuries at least. Even in the far reaches of the globe, we stick to ancient recipes instead of allowing spores of change to take the dumpling through another gastronomic leap.

Memory Capsules

Mothers are pack rats. Even when I reached my twenties, my mother continued to save the ultra-fine clothes I wore as a newborn, kiddy birthday dresses, anklets and other things I had long since outgrown.

Doris, Rom's mother, was even worse. She saved not only Rom's kiddy clothes, baby shoes, toys and books, but also his scribbles and artistic endeavours. Soon after Rom and I got together, these things began to trickle into our home.

First to arrive was a tyrannosaurus rex five-year-old Rom had fashioned with plasticine clay. Over years of sitting out on the sideboard, the clay figurine was gouged by potter wasps to make their own nests. The other day, my Lady Friday knocked it sideways and its crest detached itself. I can't shake off the feeling of guilt. Doris had saved it impeccably in tissue for more than 40 years, while in our custody it was falling apart piece by piece.

Another souvenir of Rom's childhood was a little wooden pig. It was a present from four-year-old Rom's little friend, Maggie, the daughter of jazz musician, Eddie Condon. Maggie and Rom went to the same St Luke's School in Greenwich Village in New York and were playmates. The little pig, now missing its feet, is the only reminder of Maggie.

After Doris died, more of these markers of Rom's growing-up years came home. There were many colourful drawings of snakes, lizards and fanciful beasts of Rom's imagination. This was followed by numerous letters written from boarding school describing school life interspersed with requests for 45 RPM records, jeans cut a particular style, slacks with a buckle in the back, and shirts with button-down collars.

Recently, Rom's cousin, John Babson, proved himself to be another hoarder. He sent us a scan of a letter he had received as a five-year-old and was down with measles. It was sent by seven-year-old Rom soon after arriving in India in 1951.

In the letter, Rom described his voyage across the world on the ocean liner S.S. Independence, as well as first impressions of his adopted homeland. He narrated buying a carved soapstone turtle when anchored at Gibraltar. He lowered dollars in a little basket to the vendor bobbing in a small dinghy next to the ship. More than 60 years later, that turtle sits on the sideboard with the clay dinosaur and wooden pig.

In Colaba, in the city of Bombay, little Rom found anemones, moray eels, and colourful tropical fish in tidal pools. 'Outside our porch here there is a whole row of banana trees and it seems as tho' the bananas are growing upside down,' the seven-year-old wrote. Today, the tidal pools are dead, and one would be hard put to find a banana tree.

Recently, Rom pointed out I was no less of a pack rat. I saved various little things that once belonged to our pets, like collars. When dogs grow up, the size of their collars reminds me how tiny they once were. I guess our mothers derived the same sense of wonderment from these souvenirs, memory capsules of their kids.

Some reminders are sombre. After our German shepherd, Karadi, had been killed by a leopard, all we recovered were bones and a few long hairs. Those hairs, saved in an envelope, are a sad reminder of a much-loved pet.

It's not only mothers; we are all pack rats by nature. Of things, but more importantly, memories.

The Frog Call Quiz

'Hear that faint little *payn payn*? What's that?' demanded Rom with all the exacting authority of a schoolmaster.

I concentrated for a few minutes to pick out the right frequency from the racket and ventured hesitantly, 'Ramanella?'

'No. Try again.'

'Uh . . . Fergusoni?'

'No, of course not.'

It was the first night of the monsoon, and a zillion horny male frogs and toads were croaking loudly and insistently. Faint, high, squeaky notes vied with loud, insistent ones, while deep, low-pitched calls punctuated the din. To Rom, it was a complete big band orchestra to be savoured, individually identified and enjoyed. He is so animal-fixated that he presumes I share his obsession.

At that moment, all I wanted to do was sleep.

It was past 10 at night and we were both lying in bed, wide awake from the cacophony. A pond next to the house was the arena of amphibian sex so we had unenviable high fidelity, surround sound with subwoofers and supertweeters. The air reverberated so much even my ear plugs throbbed in time with the racket and I pulled them out. I suffered both – the froggie calls to mate and my mate's persistent tutorial on frog croaks. I knew, however, both would shut up in a couple of days. We went through this torturous ritual at the same time last year, the year before and the decade before that.

I gave up. 'I don't remember. What is it?'

'But there are only 14 species. How hard is it to remember?'

'It's not as if they call everyday,' I wailed. 'The last time they did was a year ago.'

'Tomopterna. Hear that insistent *bek bek bek*? That's Uperodon.'

Even as I listened to Rom with one ear, I was wondering how to shut the frogs up. Elsewhere, near forest areas, they were nervous of lights. Here, I've shone Rom's powerful 5,00,000 candlepower spotlight, but the blighters were too much in the throes of ardent rut to even pause. One sleepless night, I even yelled at them. All I got was a two-second respite. Just a couple of days more, I consoled myself.

In the middle of the lesson on frog calls, I must have fallen asleep.

When I woke up, the volume had turned down considerably, and I half-expected Rom to drone, 'That *bwaap bwaap*. . . .' Instead he was snoring, perhaps jamming with frogs in his dreams. It was still dark and I lay there wondering why I couldn't remember these calls.

When Rom woke up, I told him my aural memory was poor and there was no point in testing it. Even with music, I can't remember who sang a particular song.

'But you learnt to recognize birds by their song. So what's your problem with frogs?'

I nodded.

Experts kept changing frog names so often that perhaps I had given up not only on their names but their calls too. The truth is, I learnt birdsong when Rom and I were courting, and I was out to impress him. Mission accomplished, I had become a lazy slob.

The next evening, as the frog chorus started up, I let out a long-suffering martyr's moan.

That's when Rom made the astounding claim that deafening frog croaks caused the French Revolution. The swamps around Paris were so full of frogs which called all night that the aristocracy couldn't sleep. They had serfs whacking the water hard to stop the amphibians from calling. If any frog so much as peeped, the poor people had hell to pay. The sleepless folk decided enough was enough and revolted.

Smug in his wisdom, Rom concluded, 'Thus the Revolution was born.'

Obviously, a desperate adult had tried to get school-boy Rom to pay attention to history lessons.

I said, 'Good story, but utter nonsense.'

'And that's why the French are called "frogs".'

'If you find a reference to that story, I promise I'll learn frog calls.'

I may have silenced at least the quiz master.

Rom, Snakes, and Ray's Tales

I was reading Satyajit Ray's *The Mystery of Nayan*, and was pleased when detective Feluda and his entourage arrived in Madras. It is so gratifying to read a story in which the action is set in one's own hometown.

Then I drew my breath sharply in surprise. Ray wrote, 'It had been decided that we'd go to the Snake Park today. An American called Whitaker had created it and, by all accounts, it was certainly worth a visit.'

Encountering one's partner in a work of fiction, written by no less than Satyajit Ray himself, has to rate as super cool.

As a young film student, I had idolized Ray. Naturally. I studied his shots and storyboard, his use of music and art direction. But his Feluda adventure series had long been inaccessible as Ray wrote in Bengali. Recently, our auditor-friend, Vishwanathan handed me a two-volume anthology: *The Complete Adventures of Feluda* published in English. He had no idea Rom was featured in one of the stories.

A couple of pages later, I read, 'We didn't spend very long in the Snake Park, but even a short visit showed us what a unique place it was. It seemed incredible that a single individual had planned the whole thing. I saw every species of snake that I had read about, and many that I didn't know existed. The park itself was beautifully designed, so walking in it was a pleasure.'

My initial excitement gave way to disappointment. Neither Rom nor the Snake Park played a defining role in the chain of dramatic events in the story. Surely Ray could have found many ways of getting either Feluda or the villain, a magician, in a jam with the numerous reptilian residents of the park.

I asked Rom about Ray's visit. 'It was in early 1980s, I think. His fascination for snakes was obvious. As I showed him around, he kept saying what beautiful and graceful animals they were. He said he wanted to make a film with snakes and I said I'd be happy to help him. But nothing ever came of it.'

Satyajit Ray had worked with a snake nearly three decades earlier in his most famous film, *Pather Panchali*. Towards the end of the movie, a black snake crawls into the hut of the main character, the young Apu. The shot held foreboding menace, and then when Ray cut to the tragedy-stricken family leaving in a bullock cart, it was clear none of them would return.

A few years prior to making his masterpiece, Ray assisted the French filmmaker, Jean Renoir, in the film *The River*. In it, a little English boy growing up in Bengal tries to 'charm' cobras by playing a flute and dies of snakebite. When the movie was released in 1951, Rom's family, half way across the world, was about to embark on a voyage to India. Though only seven years old, Rom was already catching snakes, and now his parents intended to set him loose in the Land of Snakes. His grandparents and aunts became extremely anxious on seeing their worst nightmare confirmed on screen. Eventually they grew accustomed to Rom's offbeat profession.

Although he had set up reptile conservation organizations, by the late 1980s Rom was earning a living from filmmaking. In the early 1990s, he teamed up with filmmakers, Carol and Richard Foster, to produce a film. That was the first wildlife documentary I worked on. During the interminable shoot, Richard revealed that he had played the boy who died of cobra bite in Renoir's movie. The story had come full circle.

Had I written a fictional screenplay of the influence this cast of personalities, involving Ray, Renoir, Richard, and Rom (even their names begin with R), had on each other, my scriptwriting professor would have considered it bad form. I can hear him say, 'The story has to follow an internal logic. Avoid resorting to so many coincidences.' But who is to tell life that?

Sting in the Tale

That evening, Momo didn't curl up under my table as she normally did. Instead, she lay down beside me. When I shut down my computer, the little dog sat up and looked pointedly at my bare feet. There was a scorpion inches away. I scooped it up on a piece of paper and flung it out the door.

This wasn't the first or last scorpion to be found in the house. Occasionally, we find the large, greenish-black, forest scorpion wandering across the floor. The Irula tribesmen don't take them seriously, so I've learnt not to be awed by their size or theatrically threatening display. Rarely, we find a stumpy, metallic black species whose identity I haven't pinned down. But the Indian red scorpion is more numerous and the one we fear the most.

The Reds make themselves comfortable in open bookshelves, nestling in the depression between hardcovers. Tiled and thatched roofs also make perfect scorpion hide-outs. When the creatures come out of crevices to hunt at night, they fall down on sleeping humans, and sometimes, sting. A lot of children are known to die every year, their small bodies unable to resist the potent venom.

The vast majority of scorpion stings are non-fatal, but extremely painful. On the victim's arm, Rom places iodine and citric acid crystals, and adds a drop of water. The chemical reaction causes bubbling, a wisp of smoke to rise and sharp pain. This dramatic show doesn't neutralize the venom; it's a psychological trick, a placebo. The victim experiences instant relief from intense pain.

Ironically, after years of living peacefully with Reds at home, I ran into one in the wild. Some years ago, a few friends, Rom and I camped on the sandy banks of River Denwa, Madhya Pradesh. Next morning, after breakfast, we began packing to leave. I was barefoot and planned to put on my shoes after we crossed the river. Suddenly, I fell forward, a sharp pain shooting from my little toe. There had been no thorns about, and I looked around, puzzled. Sticking up out of the sand was the raised tail of a scorpion. Until then, I would never have thought of finding a scorpion at that time and at that place.

Rom scooped it up; it was a Red. Clearly I had stepped on it, pushing its whole body under the sand, and the critter had stung in self-defence. Others were concerned, but I was confident I was in no danger. It was an extremity, farthest away from the heart, and I wasn't a child. I just had to give the venom time to work its way into my system and be metabolized. As the pain crept up my leg, I thought one of us could have been stung on the face in our sleep. Scary thought.

The entire leg throbbed, I couldn't bear to touch it or even rest it on the ground. When everyone was ready to go, I hobbled using a stick as a crutch. Wading across the cold Denwa took the pain to greater heights. I wasn't sure if I would be able to climb up the steep slope. But there was no alternative way of getting out. Where was Rom's magic crystal kit when I needed it?

Golak, one of our friends, had a bad knee and was carrying painkillers. I popped a couple and slowly made the long climb up to civilization. I was totally fine and free of pain in 24 hours.

A few months later, I described the experience to a doctor-friend who specializes in tropical medicine, and he was aghast at my nonchalance. Rom and I hadn't known the Red's venom can cause life-threatening complications, affecting the lungs and heart, even in adults. Some venom specialists consider the Red the deadliest scorpion in the world.

Momo is smart to be vigilant, unlike me, her sometimes dumb and blind Mamma.

Summertime

Every year, as summer progresses, the rising heat becomes the focal point of conversation. Friends emerge from air-conditioned rooms only to moan and groan. Visitors from other cities, especially Delhi where summers are as mild as on the planet Mercury, complain, 'Oh, Madras is so hot.'

Out here on the farm, summer is a festival of colours, sounds, scents, and tastes. The hot weather, which sends some of our friends fleeing to cooler climes, seems to make a whole range of plants and creatures feel sexy. The beginning of the sweaty season smells of neem.

Rom couldn't have chosen a better moment to propose. It was a particularly beautiful evening; the moon was full and the scent of numerous neem trees in full bloom had already made me feel giddy. I was a goner.

After neem, it's the turn of the extravagant and sweet-smelling yellow blooms of laburnum. After a few days of providing delight, the petals drop, and long, phallic, green pods dangle from trees.

By early May, the farm smells of honey, the fragrance of numerous myrobalan flowers. When neem and jamun fruits ripen, birds go crazy, chirping, gorging, pooping, fighting, mating, and rearing babies. Melodious birdsong rises to a crescendo during the soporific afternoons.

In early April, the magpie-robins furtively scout the eaves for nesting sites. If they catch us looking in their direction, they scoot away like they've been up to mischief. However, if they do nest in the roof, their shyness vanishes. The parents become flying devils, dive bombing us and screaming hoarse curses.

We become interlopers in our own home. Even though there is no threat of rain, I leave the house with an unfurled umbrella to shield my head from these avian monsters, or I make a dash for safety beyond the birds' territory. The dogs are harried the worst, and they slink away with tails tucked and heads held low.

Even the normally sluggish crocs at the Croc Bank go into reproductive overdrive. Egg laying starts in February and a few stragglers are still at it even now. When we lived at the Bank, I was up early toiling hard with the rest of the crew, digging up eggs laid during the night and ferrying them to the incubator. As I passed Rom's office, I would hear him sing the Beatles' song, 'I am the Egg Man'. That strange, psychedelic song was both anthem and earworm for the season. By the end of the morning, when all the eggs had been marked, checked for fertile embryos and tucked into incubators, I was sweaty and completely exhausted.

Reptiles, such as crocs and turtles, are dependent on warm weather in more ways than one. Since these animals don't sit on their eggs like birds do, external warmth is essential for embryo growth. More importantly, heat decides whether the hatchling will be a boy or a girl. In humans, the Y chromosome dictates our gender. But crocs and turtles have no sex chromosome.

This is how it works. Croc eggs incubated at lower and higher temperatures produce girls. Boys are formed in the in-between range. Dr Jeffrey Lang conducted a nine-year research project at the Croc Bank on the subject, and today we can produce any sex ratio by flipping the thermostat on the incubator.

That's not all. Since crocs are cold-blooded, they get warm by lying in the sun. Boy and girl crocs incubated on the warmer side choose to bask for longer, getting hotter than their siblings incubated at lower temperatures. The 'hot' animals digest their food faster, get hungry earlier, and want to eat oftener. The result? They grow faster and bigger. Large bull crocs have an edge over smaller males, while large females produce more eggs.

It makes reproductive sense to be hot whether it's a neem tree, magpie-robin or a crocodile.

Or humans.

The Taming of the Shrew

'We got a shrew,' announced Rom, one morning.

I peered into the garbage can. The little grey creature, its long, quivering nose pointed at me, sat amongst shredded pieces of paper.

'What are you going to do with it?' I asked.

'Take it far away.'

'But why? It probably lives here. Remember, I told you I saw one zip along the kitchen wall and duck under the sideboard a few days ago? It may be the same fellow, no?'

'A house is no place for a rodent.'

'It's not a rodent. It's an insectivore.'

'All right. It's a bloody rodent-like insectivore. It will chew into everything.'

'It didn't chew up anything. See, the bowl of potatoes on the counter is untouched.'

'That's because it can't climb.'

'But there's no food on the floor. The cupboards are closed. So why don't you let it be?'

'No, no, no. It can chew the gas cylinder's hose pipe, electrical wires, anything. It's destructive.'

'But it can't climb, so how can it bite the pipe or wires? It's no use arguing with you. I'll probably want to write about shrews for the column, so let me get a picture first.'

Rom emptied the laundry basket, half-filled it with dirt, and transferred the shrew. The little thing flung itself against the walls, sometimes almost high enough to get away. When it wasn't leaping, it ran along the plastic wall. Occasionally, it sat still enough for a shot, but its nose wouldn't stop trembling.

Rom said, 'It's ravenous. What can I feed it?'

Earlier, I had seen a grasshopper on a windowsill in the porch. When Rom dropped the insect close by, the shrew pounced on it and clamped down on its neck. Now that the creature had something to do, it paid us no attention at all. I placed the camera centimetres away from the shrew and clicked away.

Once the shrew and I were done, Rom released the creature into the garden.

'It will be back for sure. Remember those tree frogs we moved a kilometre away? They came back. What's 20 metres for a shrew?' I asked smugly.

One evening, many years ago, I watched a mother shrew lead her three babies around our back porch. Since they are almost blind, one baby held on to its mother's tail with its mouth, while the next in line held on to the first baby's tail, and the third had a hold of the second one's tail.

I wonder if the English rhyme, 'Three blind mice', refers to shrews. Cutting off their tails would be the cruelest thing to do to these creatures.

The babies didn't trip on each other's tails, tread on one another's feet, or stop to scratch. They kept up with their mother so well that the 'caravaning' foursome looked like one long, lumpy snake. It was one of the cutest sights to behold.

A long time ago, Rom stepped on a shrew by mistake, and was bitten. This difference in our experiences probably explains the polarity of our attitudes.

Many people are revolted by shrews. The public image of these poor creatures needs an overhaul. Bad body odour is partly to blame. What puts people off also puts most predators off. Precisely the trick for a morsel-sized mammal to survive. But shrews musk only during certain times of the year. While we were taking photographs and bothering the animal, it didn't stink at all.

The other misfortune to befall shrews is their resemblance to rodents. Shrews are not rats; they are not even related. They are insectivores, and useful allies in maintaining a pest-free kitchen.

A few days after the shrew was evicted, I found one in the same garbage can. I dumped it out on the kitchen floor, and watched it scoot under the sideboard.

What Rom doesn't know can't bother him.

Animal Suicide

Do animals commit suicide? Rom has regaled almost everyone we know with his animal suicide stories.

In the 1970s, Rom and his Irula buddy, Rajamani were looking for reptiles in Sengeltheri, in what was later to become Kalakkad-Mundanthurai Tiger Reserve. One early morning, Rom was brushing his teeth, when he saw a stork-billed kingfisher perched on a tree branch overlooking the water. Suddenly it dove straight down, and then to Rom's amazement, it lay on the water surface, wings flapping. Rom jumped from rock to rock, and when he reached the bird, it was dead. Blood oozed from its mouth. The kingfisher had hit an underwater rock.

I remembered this story recently and contended, 'That's not suicide; it was an accident.'

'Possibly. A really stupid thing for à kingfisher to do. But the treepie did take its own life.'

Rom was swimming in the sea off the Croc Bank one afternoon. A rufous treepie flew straight out from the Bank, as if it was headed to the Andaman Islands. Suddenly, it dove down into a wave, about 10 metres in front of Rom. By the time he picked the bird up, it had drunk a lot of water. It flapped weakly and wheezed, opening and closing its mouth. Standing on a sand bar, Rom tried to give it mouth-to-mouth resuscitation. 'Its breath smelt rank,' he recalls with a grimace. Despite administering CPR, the bird gave up the ghost in his hands, and Rom let it float away.

Rom asked, 'Why would a treepie fly straight out over the sea if not to commit suicide?'

Why would any animal want to kill itself? Over the years, accounts of animal suicide reflected the prevalent values of human society, say Drs Edmund Ramsden and Duncan Wilson. For instance, Aristotle recounted the story of a stallion, who on discovering he had mated with his mother, flung himself off a cliff. Shades of *Oedipus Rex*?

According to Iberian folklore, when surrounded by flames, scorpions sting themselves to death. In 1883, psychologist Conwy Lloyd Morgan conducted various scientific but horrific experiments, and exposed this as a mere folktale.

Humans have attributed numerous reasons – age, despair, grief, jealousy, desperation, captivity, cruelty, insanity, self-sacrifice through maternal or social affection, or sheer ennui. These are the very same reasons why people commit suicide.

Animals do sacrifice their lives for the greater good of their species. Male mantids offer themselves as food to their ravenous mates while mating. Bees commit hara-kiri when they sting any animal that threatens their hives; their guts spill out when the stinger is pulled out. These actions don't rate as suicide as they are hardwired into the insects' behaviour. What about rats infected with the protozoan, Toxoplasma gondii, that throw themselves under the noses of cats? This also doesn't rate as suicide as the rat is helplessly under the control of the parasite.

In his book, *Myths about Suicide*, psychologist Thomas Joiner lists three aspects in the suicidal tendencies of humans – a strong motivation to kill oneself, the belief that one's life is worth more dead than alive, and a sense of alienation from family and community.

To be suicidal, an animal should be capable of deliberation, planning, and decision-making. But first, it has to recognize itself as an individual entity. So far only higher mammals like elephants, primates, and sea mammals appear to be self-aware.

The treepie belongs to the crow family, among the smartest of the bird world. European magpies, also of the same family, have proven to be self-aware. As innovative problem solvers, New Caledonian crows are even better than chimpanzees. The birds are capable of fashioning and using tools in ingenious ways to fish food from difficult situations. If cleverness runs in the family, the treepie may well be capable of committing suicide. Or it may have been disoriented or sick.

We'll never know since it didn't leave a suicide note.

Palmyra Enigma

Wherever I've seen the palmyra along tank bunds, beaches, and degraded hillocks around here in Chengalpattu, it seems to have been planted by humans. What is its original home? To which forest type does it belong? I've spent many years walking in circles around these questions.

In his *Dictionary of the Economic Products of India*, Sir Joseph D. Hooker wrote of the palmyra, 'I believe this palm is nowhere wild in India; and have always suspected that it, like the tamarind, was introduced from Africa.' I latched on to that fragment. Sir Hooker ought to know since he conducted extensive botanical surveys in India during the mid-1800s.

However, some years ago, Rom and I found a life-like sandstone sculpture of a palmyra crown at the Jabalpur Museum. It was at least 1,500 years old. South Indians have written on strips of dried palm leaf since the 5th century BCE. Was Hooker mistaken? Perhaps palmyra was Indian but had lost its wild habitat to human settlement completely.

As a child, I crafted windmills with palmyra leaf, and the fruits made perfect wheels for carts. On numerous summer afternoons, I scooped out the tender kernel with my thumb into my greedy mouth. I drank the freshly tapped sap as a child and the fermented version as an adult. In winter months, boiled roots were sought-after snacks.

When probing into palmyra's origins didn't yield any further tidbits, I focused on another palm tree, the talipot. The word, *thali* (*mangalsutra* in South Indian languages), comes from the name of the tree, because the original wedding practice was to dip the leaf in saffron water before the groom tied it around the bride's neck. So says William Logan in his *Malabar Manual* of 1887.

However, the talipot belongs to wet forests of the west coast. In arid Tamil Nadu, it grows in temples where it was most definitely planted. It flowers once, when the tree is anywhere between 30 and 80 years old, and dies. Comparatively, the palmyra flowers and fruits every year and lives a great many years. Talipot's leaves were also used as writing material. Perhaps Tamilians originally used the native talipot, and later switched to the more fecund palmyra.

Borassus flabellifer, the palmyra's scientific name, is listed as a characteristic tree of the tropical dry evergreen forest in most botanical inventories. But it does not tolerate shade. Is it really a forest species?

I called Pradip Krishen, a tree aficionado friend. He confirmed that his reference books said palmyra was a native of the Indian subcontinent. The seed of doubt was too deeply embedded in my head to accept that unconditionally.

I started the search from the other end, Africa. Palmyra grows all across that continent's savannas. It truly seemed at home there, surrounded by giraffes, zebras, elephants and other animals. The only creatures I've seen ambling around these palms here are cows and goats. Then it hit me. I was looking at *Borassus aethiopum*, and one of its other names was *Borassus flabellifer*. The World Agroforestry Centre suggests that the African species may have been domesticated and became the Indian palmyra. Years of selective breeding may have created a new species, just as domesticated wolves became dogs.

Excited by this discovery, I e-mailed another friend, Rohan Pethiyagoda, who shares my interest in history. Within hours, he sent me a scientific paper that showed our palmyra was a distinct species in its own right, even though it looks almost identical to aethiopum. The former ranges across the Indian subcontinent and into the Malayan peninsula while the latter was strictly African. But that doesn't resolve the question of palmyra's origin. Prehistoric trade could have dispersed a domesticated species far and wide, especially if it had many uses. Rohan says a genetic study currently underway will resolve the ambiguity.

Until then, I just have to learn to be patient.

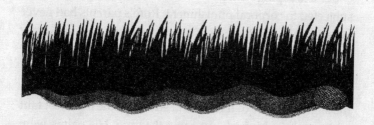

Harin Chattopadhyaya's
Birthday Poem

I was thinking of birthday present ideas. Rom and his sister, Gail, turn a year older in May.

The special session of Parliament held in early May 2012 also reminded me that 60 years ago, Harindranath Chattopadhyaya, Rom's step-grandfather, took his seat in the country's first Lok Sabha as an Independent representing Vijayawada. That year Rom was sent to Lawrence School in Ooty.

Besides coping with home-sickness, the nine-year-old was subjected to corporal punishment. Rom's parents had never raised their hands against their children, and suddenly becoming a victim of physical violence traumatized him.

Rom was the lone white kid in a 600-strong school, and he felt his teachers took special delight in punishing him on the slightest pretext. If he hadn't stretched the bedsheet taut while making his bed, out came the cane. His palms were swollen and painful, and angry red welts erupted across his calves from the caning.

Rom wrote letters full of misery to his mother in Bombay,

letters she was never to receive. He cried himself to sleep, hurt as much by the public humiliation as the physical pain. His mother wrote to him regularly, never acknowledging his struggles in school. Rom became despondent thinking she had abandoned him to this hell.

When Rom was slumped into depression, Granddaddy Harindranath arrived unannounced. Within minutes, the jovial, fun-loving grandfather turned wrathful. He thundered against the school's child abuse. Promising retribution, he took Breezy, as the family called Rom, back to Bombay.

More than a parliamentarian, Harin is best remembered as a poet. Perhaps his most popular poem is 'Rel gaadi chook chook, chook chook'. When I was thinking of the upcoming birthdays, I recalled a poem Granddaddy Harin wrote 64 years ago.

A Birthday Poem for Gale and Breezy

Two children on their natal day awaken
To find that they are a year older than
They were a year ago . . . .
To them I send my greetings glad and warm,
The poet-father of a grown-up man,
Ramu – who says Breezy and Gale have taken
His heart by storm:
Now, tell me, Gale and Breezy, is that so?

Yes! Warmest greetings from my poet's pen
To Gale who has this day completed nine
Which means, next year, this day, she will be ten,
So, once again this rhyming pen of mine

Will have to write at least another line
Of equally warm greeting . . . .
Now, little girl! Though time be ever fleeting
May everyone around you say: 'To Gale
Life always seems a rainbowed fairy tale
Since she has got the knack of lending wings
To the most foolish, ordinary things.'

And now, we come to Breezy-Boy, alive
And kicking at the tender age of five.
A favourite pastime with him, I declare,
Is 'Come on, Ramu, "trow" me in the air!'
A charming lad who, under a magic wand,
Became a blue-eyed angel-boy – and blonde!
His one desire of all his keen desires
Is just to meddle with electric wires.
(Which often gives the home a shock or two
Far greater than electric wires do!)
But he himself needs none, the little scamp,
Since he himself is an electric lamp,
Self-kindled with a joy that never tires
Without the help of long electric wires!

God bless you both, my loves! God bless you both
And bless your education and – your growth!

Harindranath was the only grandfather Rom really had. He
had no contact with his father's family, and after moving to
India, he had no physical contact with his mother's parents.
By the time he completed school and went to the States to
attend university, his maternal grandparents had passed
away. Granddaddy Harin taught the kids Tagore songs,

narrated nonsensical stories, made up crazy limericks, and indulged them with chocolates and gifts.

What presents to give Rom and Gail on their birthdays? No matter what I think up, I'm sure it will not measure up to this poem.

Evolution by Fire

When Rom and I started living together, I didn't know how to cook. Rom made sandwiches, and occasionally a stew. After a while, I just couldn't handle sandwiches anymore. I wanted real food. Perhaps concerned by our diet, Doris, Rom's mom, gave us a much-used *The Fanny Farmer Cookbook*, first published in 1906.

Fanny Farmer merely boiled, buttered, salted, and peppered her vegetables. It was so simple, but locally-available produce like lablab, gourds, lady's fingers, cluster beans prepared in that style tasted vile. Forget home delivery or takeaway; there was no restaurant in a 40 km radius. If I wanted to eat, I had to cook. I bought a stack of recipe books, a sack of veggies, and set to work. And that's how I found myself performing a traditional woman's role – cooking.

I was thinking of those early days while reading primatologist Richard Wrangham's book, *Catching Fire: How Cooking Made Us Human*.

For a long time, scientists have puzzled over what significant change in diet led to developing our large brains. The grey mass guzzles as much as a quarter of the body's energy. Until now, paleontologists were hedging their bets on a meat diet. But other ape-like ancestors ate meat with no corresponding increase in brain size.

Wrangham says the answer is cooked tubers. Fire releases hard-to-digest nutrients, neutralizes toxins, and reduces the amount of time we spend chewing. In comparison, our raw-food eating primate cousins spend all day munching. Wringing more calories from cooked food shrank our digestive tracts, and the saved energy powered our large brains. And made us human.

When Wrangham's book came out in 2004, primatologists and paleontologists contested it. They said cooking as a widespread cultural event was only about 2,50,000 years old. For Wrangham's theory to hold, Prometheus had to have stolen fire from the heavens 1.8 million years ago, not for Homo sapiens or Neanderthals but Homo erectus. But the earliest confirmed proof of cooking is only a million years old.

Could Homo erectus have survived without fire? Unable to process starch, he would have needed a high-fat, high-protein diet. In the Middle East, the survival of these ancient humans was tied to eating elephants, say Israeli scientists.

Not only Homo erectus, even some modern humans do live without processing their food by fire. In recent times, a raw food diet has become a fad. The idea that naturally occurring nutrients are destroyed by fire drives this philosophy of eating.

In Arunachal Pradesh, we carried power bars on our hikes, while our Nishi guide, Taka picked a variety of leaves, roots, and flowers along the way. At break time, he rinsed his bouquet in a fast-flowing stream, seasoned it with salt and pepper, and his snack was ready to eat. Soon I was following his example. Salad is all right for a snack, but I still need wholesome cooked food suitably spiced.

In Auroville, a farmer-friend, who had just milked his cow, handed me a glass of frothy fresh milk. Since the time I was little, my mother has always boiled milk. The fear of bovine-borne disease is so deeply ingrained I wasn't sure how to react to the glass in my hand. Reading my mind, our friend reassured me, 'The cows are certified disease-free. Go on, taste it.' The raw milk was delicious, like ice-cream. But I wouldn't try unboiled milk anywhere else.

After Prometheus committed the crime of giving fire to men, Zeus sent Pandora, the first woman, to earth in retaliation. She is supposed to have unleashed evil upon the world, but she also collected tubers and tended the hearth. The division of labour along gender lines is still prevalent in human society. Men hunt, while women cook.

Occasionally I fancy becoming a raw food-itarian, just to escape the chore of cooking. Salmonella-infested raw eggs or masala omelette? Raw unpalatable brinjal or *baingan barta*? Gooey batter or baked brownies? I've become a slave of my tastebuds, thanks to fire.

An Airboat Adventure in Papua

How to look for crocodile nests in swamps where no boat can penetrate? Salvinia, the waterweed from South America, choked all channels of the River Sepik, Papua New Guinea. The matted vegetation was so thick that it was impossible to use boats. Alistair Graham, Rom's colleague on the croc project, came up with an idea – airboat.

Old-timers in Florida will tell you, 'All an airboat needs is a bit of dew to slide over land.' It was perfect for the work on hand. Weeks later, an airboat arrived at Madang on the Northern coast of the country. Alistair and Rom had to deliver it to Ambunti, a tiny village on the Sepik. That meant a two-day ride of over a 100 kms in the sea. But airboats are meant for swamp use, not open, choppy waters. There was no other way of transporting it except by driving it along the coast.

One early morning, the two set off with the smoking Manam volcano on one side and the coast on the other. People tumbled out of coastal towns and villages and lined the shore to see this strange beast. The airplane engine created a huge racket, while a spectacular water plume arched out of the rear end. Although none of the villagers had seen an airboat before, they promptly named it *balus* boat ('airplane boat' in English) in inimitable Pidgin, the country's lingua franca.

Moments later, the wind direction changed and blew the water plume into the boat, swamping it. So while one of the two adventurers sat regally and drove the airboat, the other was stooped over, feverishly pumping out water with a little fuel hand pump, and feeling sick from the exhaust fumes. It was no ride in a pond. The faster they went, the more water swamped the boat. They took turns at the pump, but still it was a slow chug. Sailfish flashed their sails in threat at this strange beast on the water.

That evening, at dusk, they saw a light in a beautiful cove, and a crowd of people waving at them. It seemed as good a place as any to spend the night. The spectators were from a copra plantation run by an Australian who invited them for a beer and steak dinner, and even gave them a room for the night.

It took them all of the next day to reach the mouth of the Sepik. At the estuary, the boat was surrounded by a hundred sea snakes. Since the river was like glass, Alistair opened up the throttle and planed across the water.

Within seconds, they hit a mud bank and almost flipped over. Thick mangroves, numerous saltwater crocodiles, no help for miles in the event of an accident. It could have been a disaster. Shaken, they drove upriver, careful to avoid solid mud banks, but glided over logs, debris, and salvinia effortlessly.

Three days after setting off from Madang and more than 200 kms later, they arrived in Ambunti. For the next two years, the airboat would be used to survey one of the remotest parts of the world for crocodile nests, where no man had tread or boated in a long time.

Twenty years later, Rom and I visited Ambunti. After a couple of days and nights of going up and down the river looking for crocs, one taciturn young man asked Rom quietly, 'Were you the one who brought the balus boat?' A surprised Rom answered, 'Yes! But how do you know? You must have been very young then.' Others, young and old, also piped up. After narrating the story, Rom concluded, 'It's one of the craziest things I've done in my life.'

In Papua New Guinea, stories are carved on panels of wood called 'storyboards' in the art market. Since I can't carve, here is the word-story of the balus boat that conquered salvinia on the Sepik.

Indians Gone Potty

Jackals mark their territories by defecating on prominent sites like boulders. Civets do it on the run, especially along fallen logs. Rhinos have community latrines; several of them visit the same spot to deposit their dung. Gharials like to evacuate in water.

Hundreds of millions of Indians, like jackals, flamboyantly leave unsightly piles out in the open; some park their vehicles and do it on the roadside, not unlike civets; others, like rhinos, prefer latrines. But disastrously, millions more turn freshwater bodies such as lakes, springs, rivers, and canals into toilets.

Never has the want of a toilet terrorized me as much as the trip I made through a rural district in Maharashtra in early 2005. Over three days, I talked to families of victims who had been attacked by leopards. I heard stories of terror, disabilities, and bereavement.

During the course of the day, tall crops such as sugarcane, banana, and corn provided ample cover to relieve oneself, just as some of the victims had when the shadow of death fell on them. I ducked behind these plants nervously; it took just a leaf moving in a whisper of wind or a sudden distant sound to make me jump. When I sought the privacy of one dark banana plantation, the nearby temple loudspeaker was so loud that had I screamed in distress, no one would have heard. If I was so tense in broad daylight when hardly any leopards were around, it must have been utter terror for villagers when the cats were out prowling in the dark.

Several villages in this sugar bowl of Maharashtra appeared prosperous. Yet, even the largest houses didn't have toilets. That's no surprise. Even in my village in Tamil Nadu, the richest landowner who owns a SUV, tractor, harvester, and about 30 acres of irrigated land has no toilet in his house. Every morning, his family lines up along our shared boundary and defecates in the open. In leopard-land, a few households that had lost a family member to the big cats had completely renovated their houses with the compensation money they received from the government. But no toilets were added.

If lack of indoor plumbing put people in danger, you'd think they would change their behaviour. But the taboo of human waste in the house runs so deep that even the threat to human life wasn't enough incentive to build a toilet. If en suite loos were forbidden, why not make outhouses? I lacked the language and skill to ask these delicate questions.

On the last day, I finally found a row of toilets in one village. But there was no water to flush, and a radius of 50 metres around the loos was a disgusting open latrine. A five-year-old girl had been killed a few feet away. While the father was narrating the horrific sequence of events, I was trying not only to ignore the awful stench but unobtrusively ward off the clouds of flies.

Returning to base every evening, closing the toilet door, and being able to relax felt like a guilty to-die-for luxury.

Since I'm programmed to go to a pre-assigned area, I'm like a rhino I guess. But I'm also more like a cat that fastidiously buries its poop. Urbanized rhino-cats like me are quick to feel superior to rural India's jackal ways. We wonder what it would take to convert the unwashed masses to our way of doing things. Subsidies, exhortations by movie stars, cheap toilets?

Where does our own superior rhino-cat poop end up? Urban sanitation systems are so poorly equipped that untreated septic sludge is dumped into rivers. The faecal content in some rivers is so high, they are unfit even for bathing. We worship these waterways as goddesses and desecrate them just the same. Are we a nation of chimeras?

Is My Husband an Animal?

The commonest question readers ask is – why is my column called 'My Husband and Other Animals'?

'Notions of Nature', 'Under the Sun', 'Upfront and Wild' were some of the other contenders for the title. None of them encapsulated my style of writing and everything I wanted to write about as well as 'My Husband and Other Animals'.

Many who wrote to me thought the title was amusing, while some recognized it was in the tradition of Gerald Durrell's *My Family and Other Animals*. Others didn't get the point, and a few were outraged. One gave me a lecture on my apparent lack of respect for my husband.

Are you discomforted by the thought I consider my husband an animal? We are 96 per cent chimpanzee. I'm being provocative, of course. What I mean is we share 96 per cent of our DNA with chimps. More astonishingly, scientists have discovered almost 500 segments of human DNA that have remained totally unchanged, some of them for 400 million years, about the time our remote ancestor split from fish. We share these ancient fragments with fish, chicken, rats, and dogs. Perhaps we are animals in blood and tissue, but outclass them in brain power.

We think we are unique because we have culture. Some animals do too. A herd of moose in central Norway goes up into the higher reaches for winter, while elsewhere, moose head for lowland pastures. 5,000 years ago, the ancestors of the central region herd were hunted in pit traps, and in response, they fled upwards. Although the threat has disappeared, moose of this region continue the culture of spending winters in the high hills where food is scarce.

Is it our use of language that compels us to believe we're superior to other creatures? Most animals and birds have a form of language. Some, like dolphins and whales, have a huge vocabulary. Baby bottlenose dolphins even name themselves. When two strange dolphins meet they exchange names, like we do at conferences and parties. With each passing year, scientists studying animal cognition reveal birds and animals are smarter than we previously thought. And it's becoming harder to define what it is to be human.

We are a self-aware species, some scientists say. Robins will peck at mirrors viciously, mistaking their reflections for rivals. But elephants, apes, dolphins, and magpies groom themselves by looking at the mirror, demonstrating self-awareness. There goes another definition of human.

Is it our ability to empathize? Bonobos empathize. So do rats. But many humans don't. Sense of humour? Chimps and dogs pant with laughter. Rats chirp when tickled. Does their ability to laugh indicate an innate sense of humour? No answers yet. But I sure wish some humans had a sense of humour.

Art? Seals, ravens, and elephants paint, but we don't know yet if they intend their creations to be symbolic of the world they see. Chimps and gorillas indicate what they are painting by sign language so we know they are creating art and having fun doing it.

Are we human because we experience spirituality? The part of our brain that lights up during a spiritual experience is also present in animals. So there is no reason why they may not have similar moments. After heavy showers, primatologist Jane Goodall reported chimps dance with gay abandon at newly formed waterfalls. Some even go into a trance-like state. Later, one of them may sit on a rock, and stare at the waterfall as if mulling over the nature of water.

In trying to define what it is to be human, we invariably turn our gaze to the animal world. We are, in effect, exploring animal cognition in an effort to understand what makes us human. The more we try to set ourselves above animals, the more they demonstrate they are no different.

Whatever it means to be human, my husband is, first and foremost, an animal. And so are you and I.

ACKNOWLEDGEMENTS

It would not have been possible to write some of these articles without the help of several invaluable friends and colleagues. They provided leads, information, advice, and inspiration. Most are mentioned in the articles but some have gone unacknowledged until now.

Gopi Sundar of the International Crane Foundation was pivotal in helping me write 'A Partridge by Any Other Name'. Not only did he patiently answer my questions, he pointed me to the remarkable YouTube video of the lyrebird for 'Bird Impersonators' and sent scientific papers on anything to do with birds. Since I don't belong to an educational institution, my access to technical literature is dependent on the magnanimity of friends like Gopi. Aniruddha Belsare at the University of Missouri was another vital source of scientific literature.

While researching the long-distance movement of saltwater crocodiles in far-flung islands for 'Danger in Paradise', I relied on expert advice from Kent Vliet and James Perran Ross of the University of Florida, Christopher Brochu of the University of Iowa, and John 'Jack' Frazier of the Smithsonian Institution. Eben Goodale of the University of San Diego shared his research papers on racket-tailed drongos for 'Bird Impersonators'.

Pavithra Sankaran of Nature Conservation Foundation (NCF) remembered the late Ravi Sankaran's story of the takin in Nagaland far better than I did. T.R. Shankar Raman, also of NCF, challenged my assumptions on an earlier draft of 'Animal Suicide'.

I also received a lot of help with writing. Ever since I signed up for the Internet Writing Workshop, my writing has improved tremendously. I'm trained to be a film editor, not a writer. I wrote like I edited a movie – an abrupt cut or paragraph change to transition from one scene to the next. I didn't have enough schooling to know about misplaced modifiers and comma placements. Many participants in the workshop helped me understand the rules of grammar, punctuation, and flagged incomprehensible leaps in story.

Mukund Padmanabhan, Baradwaj Rangan, Krithika Reddy and W. Sreelalitha of *The Hindu Metroplus* are the best. Occasionally, I have made last-minute changes which they indulged with good humour. I couldn't have hoped for a better home for the column.

From the moment Westland, the publishing company, agreed to bring out the collection, it's been a frenzied period of editing, re-writing, polishing and re-structuring the articles. Aradhana Bisht and Dharini Bhaskar, the editorial team, made it all come together. Somehow.

My parents never expressed their own misgivings when I quit filmmaking. It was my second career crisis and mid-life was still some distance away. I imagine I caused more concern when I announced grandly I was going to take up writing. Despite my bravado, I wasn't sure how I was going to earn a living, and any sign of uncertainty from them would have made me feel doubly wobbly.

The one person without whom this column would not have happened is The Dude. He is subject, editor, advisor, confidante, and the first reader of anything I write. I have cancelled many dates with him because I suddenly had an idea to fix an article or write a new one. He has not only put up with sacrificing 'us-time' without a quibble, he made tea, popcorn, and plied me with glasses of wine to lubricate the writing voice in my head. More than anyone else, to him I owe who I am and what I do, quirks and all.

Thank you all.